The Spirit
of the
Limestone House

The Spirit
of the
Limestone House

Story by
Deborah Sweaney

This book is for my great nieces.

Today:
Maryjane, Lily and Nora.

Someday:
Eva, Isabella, Evelyn, Athena, Olivia and Isabelle.

Contents

List of Illustrations

Lawrence, Kansas

May 27, 2011

Callie Anne Monroe picked up the day's mail. She barely sorted it. She knew that it would contain bills, causing additional lines of worry on her mother's face. There was never enough money, no matter how hard her mother worked. It had been that way since the plane crash killed her father and grandfather two years ago.

She looked at the envelopes in her hand. She was right. The quarterly insurance payment was due. The other letter from the county must be a tax bill. However, one envelope, from a firm located in Washington, D.C., puzzled Callie. She did not think her mother had any business dealings there, but she put the envelope along with the bills in a stack for her mother.

Years later, Callie thought how casually she treated that envelope. Its contents changed her life. Callie Anne Monroe was about to learn that the past could affect the present and change her future, that death was never really the end, and above all else, that even in the twenty-first century, fairy godmothers existed.

PART

I

One

Cumberland County, PA

September 27, 2010

The news traveled fast. Amelia Calafont had died in her sleep on a cold Monday night in late September. Her housekeeper, Mamie Hodges, found her lying peacefully in her bed when she arrived at the old Calafont house Tuesday morning. Mrs. Hodges called the ambulance. By the time the emergency personnel delivered Miss Amelia's body to the undertakers, the grapevine was busy at work spreading the news that Miss Amelia Calafont was now with her maker.

It was hard to imagine that Miss Amelia had a maker and had gone through the life stages of ordinary human beings. She had looked the same for as long as anyone could remember: a small-boned woman who seemed to tower above others even though she was only five feet three inches tall. Someone once said that in her youth, her hair was a beautiful shade of dark red, but no one could recall seeing her head covered in anything but thick white hair. If asked to describe her, many might have called her an "old maid school teacher." Older folks said they could still recite fragments of the Gettysburg Address they learned in her classroom. Lincoln's speech carried special significance for them, as they knew it was delivered in Adams County, only about thirty miles from the Calafont home.

Amelia's death was hardly unexpected, but it still rattled the old-timers, as Miss Amelia Calafont had always been a part of their lives. On the Wednesday after she died, many of the town folks drove past the old Calafont place. The house sat on a slight rise facing South Mountain. The Farmers Almanac's prediction of an early fall for the Cumberland Valley was holding true. The trees were already covered with red and yellow leaves. Houses from two new developments could be seen from her front porch, but there were still fifty acres of Calafont land separating Miss Amelia's home from suburban sprawl. The original deed issued in the name of King George III to the first American Calafont described seven hundred acres, stretching from the top of the hill to the small stream called McMurphy's Run. Amelia's father sold a good portion of this land to a developer in the 1960s. It was a wise business decision, as the Calafont family made a pretty penny on the sale.

The Calafont place still caught the eye, but it needed work. No one ever doubted that Miss Amelia loved her house, but love was not enough to keep it up. For the last few years, it was clear to anyone who paid attention that the old house was getting the better of Amelia. Its deterioration coincided with her own decline. Around the time she turned 90, the paint on the old porch started to flake. Clearly, she was no longer able to take care of a home built in the same decade that settlers won their independence from England. Now one of the shutters was loose and some of the stones on the walk leading up to the house needed repairing.

It was unusual for the retired men who gathered every morning over coffee at the King's Gap General Store to agree on anything. However, none took exception when Joe Clark proclaimed, "It's an end of an era. They don't make women like Amelia Calafont anymore."

"What is going to become of the old place?" Win Hoffman pondered aloud.

They all thought that Miss Amelia was the last of her line.

Then Old Man Price asked the question that was on everyone's mind, "What's going to happen to the ghost?"

Two

Houses are not meant to be empty. They are built for living people. Now for the first time in over two hundred years, no one was residing in the old Calafont place. It was true that Mamie Hodges still opened the old house to air it out once a week; she came partly out of habit. After all, she spent twenty years taking care of Amelia Calafont and her home. It was a routine that she was unable to put aside just because Miss Amelia was gone. So, once a week, a living person was now in the house.

Mrs. Hodges' visits were Tom's only connection to the outside world. It was not by choice that his spirit had haunted the Calafont home since 1863. Tom had tried to leave, but it was not possible. His spirit was not only blocked from entering the next stage of the afterlife, but he was also unable to leave the old limestone house. He long ago abandoned any attempt at trying to figure out why this was so; it was just how it was. Now with Miss Amelia gone, he just rattled around the quiet rooms of the old house. He was all alone with only his memories for company.

These memories were all mixed together. Some captured the years before that fateful night when his physical body left him. In those memories, Tom was an active and contented participant, making a life in North Carolina with his beloved Mattie. He was a lead actor in those stories. His memories after he left his body were different. For almost a hundred fifty years, he had been a supportive player in the Calafont family drama. Now, this drama appeared to be over. It was a very serious situation. He was trapped, unable to move to the next stage, but now he could no longer observe the life of those in the present. *Is this going to be my fate for eternity?* he thought.

Tom could still smell the ginger cookies Miss Amelia baked. Of course, ghosts could not eat; they lost their taste buds when their mortal bodies left them. But for some reason that he did not try to understand, his nose and ears still worked. The smell of Miss Amelia's cookies took him back to Mattie's kitchen. Mattie baked gingerbread in her wood stove. He and Mattie ate their meals around the table in front of that stove. He could still feel her hand in his. She would place her small hand in his larger one before he said grace over the meal she prepared. She always smiled when he tickled her palm after he finished praying.

Tom remembered every detail of the house that he and Mattie called home. While the Calafont house was fancy, Tom and Mattie's was not. It was just an enlarged log cabin. Tom's grandfather cut the original logs shortly after the American Revolution, and Tom later added another bedroom and a loft. Mattie, for her part, put her own touches on the house—it was how a woman turned a house into a home. His Mattie always had a needle in her hand when she was not in her garden or kitchen and her little embroidered items adorned the main room.

Tom's mortal body left him on a hot June night in 1863. He remembered it so clearly. Tom knew that it pained Hank, his boyhood friend, to leave him in the Calafont yard.

At home, Hank's farm bordered his own small patch of land. It was sweat from his own brow that put his crops in the ground. Tom was not sure that he cottoned to the idea of owning another human being, but he was from North Carolina. He did not want the Yankees to tell him how to live, so, when Hank came by in the spring of 'sixty-one, on his way to join up, Tom went with him.

For the last several miles, Hank had been carrying Tom on his back. He was burning up with fever and it hurt to breathe. He was not fighting the effects of a musket ball—Tom had been lucky in that regard. He made it through the bloody fighting of 1862. Many of his friends died at Sharpsburg on the banks of Antietam Creek. Then, as his regiment marched into the North again, the fever grabbed him. It came on quickly. He was just barely aware that the terrain had gotten easier for the North Carolina boys as they entered the Cumberland Valley of Pennsylvania. South Mountain was behind them.

Hank told him that there were juicy apricots on the ground, but Tom was too weak to eat. Hank knew then that there was nothing he could do for his friend. When he saw the large limestone house with the trees in the front yard, he knew that if his best friend was going to die, then the peaceful yard was a better place to do so than on some battlefield.

Hank gently laid Tom down on the grass and then rejoined the troops marching onward. The soldiers did not know that in a couple of days, all hell would break loose about thirty miles away.

Sarah Calafont, Miss Amelia's great grandmother, ran out to Tom's body after Hank and the others marched on. She took her Christian duty seriously. Here was a man who needed help. It did not matter that he was invading her world. She called to thirteen-year old Matthew, her son, to help carry him into the house. She left a memory as she placed her cool hand on his fevered brow.

"What's your name, Reb?" she asked.

"Tom," he said weakly.

Sarah's gentle touch was the last human experience Tom remembered. He could hear her voice using his name. In his delirium, he called for Mattie. He heard her say, "I'm right here, Tom." He knew the woman with the kind Yankee voice was not his Mattie—even through his fever, he knew that Mattie was gone, but he found the stranger's voice pleasant and calming.

Far away from his North Carolina home, his body left him that night. He died right here in the Calafont parlor. There was no one who loved him to say good-bye when his spirit left his body. Nor did Tom have a chance to say his own good-byes. They buried his body in the Calafont family plot, next to their apple orchard. Without his last name, it was not possible to leave a proper marker or to bring closure to a life that was taken before its proper time. Just the name Tom and the date, June 29, 1863, were written on the wooden cross.

Three

Sarah Calafont never forgot the night that Tom left his physical body. It was the night that she finally cried.

She did not cry when she read the letter telling her that her husband, John, was dead. She just buried the pain someplace below her heart and worked hard. By June of 1863, John had been gone for almost two years. He died in the early days of the fighting, on a hill in Northern Virginia, by the small town of Manassas. She supposed that she was lucky. She knew John's story. The rebel musket ball hit him in the chest and he died quickly. At least that is what their neighbor, Hermann Kurtz, told her in a letter. The two men had marched off to war together, to save the Union and put down the rebellion. It was their duty. These Pennsylvania men were not going to be gone long. The war would be over soon. That is what everyone said. But the bloodshed just seemed to go on and on. The news of the fighting no longer concerned her. She thought that the war had already taken everything important. Then, the War came to Calafont land.

John had brought her to the Calafont house as a young bride. In taking his name, it became her home. She was not the first Calafont woman to live in the big limestone house. She dusted furniture that John's grandfather carted across the Susquehanna to give to his bride, the first Calafont woman to live in this house. Sarah polished the silver that had once belonged to her husband's mother and made the beds with quilts stitched by her. Because it was June, Sarah had spent the previous weeks washing the windows and cleaning the rugs. It was the tradition of the Calafont women to do the yearly cleaning in June. The spring rains were usually over by then and the men would be less likely to track mud on their clean floors. Even though there were no longer any men to mess up her house, Sarah Calafont still followed the tradition. She took the rugs out, one by one, and hung them on a line and beat the dust out of them. The Calafont house was her home, and in spite of the biblical injunction against such feelings, she was filled with pride when she looked at the limestone house.

Pride was not the only emotion that Sarah was feeling those last days of June in 1863. Fear gripped her. It was rumors that first generated the fear. Her neighbor, Levi Wertz, stopped by the house to tell her the news. Rebs were already in Shippensburg and soon would be moving down Walnut Bottom Road toward Carlisle. Upon hearing this, she and her son, Matthew, wrapped the silver in linens, and Matthew buried the large bundle in the soft dirt by the smokehouse. He then hid the cattle in King's Gap. She knew the invaders would be hungry, and she had no intention of letting them feast on Calafont cows.

Sarah stood in the yard in front of her house and listened. Loud noise had now turned the rumors into reality. The Confederates were not coming quietly like a thief in the night. You could hear them spreading out over the Cumberland Valley. They sounded closer with each passing moment. She could hear the horses, wagons, and the caissons as they approached her land. It was hot. June was turning into July. Her thick auburn hair felt heavy and tendrils escaped their bun. She could feel them on her neck. Soon the Rebel soldiers would be here. She went back inside the big house to wait for them.

Late in the afternoon, she saw the enemy first hand as she looked out the windows of the Calafont front parlor. The men did not tarry long on her land. They were moving quickly toward Carlisle. She watched as one Reb broke ranks and laid a body underneath one of her trees. When the troops disappeared around the next bend, she ran outside. She leaned over the man, expecting to find a dead body, but she jumped instead when he groaned. She stood up and for a moment thought of her husband. This man could have shot her John, but when she reached out and touched his fevered brow, she pushed the thought out of her mind. Here was a man who needed help, so she called to her son to help move the man into their home.

Sarah and Matthew put a sheet down on the settee in the parlor. Sarah did not want to put the filthy soldier directly on her furniture. Without a doubt, he was probably infected with vermin.

Sarah Calafont had treated ailing family members most of her adult life. It was what a woman did, along with cooking and mending.

She took a bowl of cool water and a cloth and wiped the sweat off the soldier's brow. She asked him his name, and when the solider weakly answered, she said it over and over again that night. In doing so, the man became a person to her. He was Tom, not just a Rebel soldier.

Sarah was unsuccessful in bringing down the soldier's fever, and in his delirious condition, she heard him say the name Mattie. She tried to comfort him by saying, "I'm right here, Tom."

Sarah did not close her own eyes that night. She stayed beside the dying man, holding his hand as the long night dragged on. The sun was just barely coming up when Tom took his last labored breath. She gently closed his eyes. Sarah was drained and her emotions on edge when she turned to his knapsack. There were two bone buttons that kept it closed. Sarah carefully unbut-

toned them. Inside were a razor, a shaving brush, a worn Bible, a daguerreotype, and a folded leather pouch.

Sarah's eyes first focused on the razor. She was not surprised that he carried one. The stubble on his cheeks was new, and she expected that the fever had kept him from his daily ablutions. His smooth face showed no sign of a mustache or other facial hair, currently favored by most men, regardless of the color of their uniform.

She picked up Tom's Bible, thinking she might find his last name. It fell open easily to the Psalms, making it clear that Tom had frequently read them. A marked passage called to Sarah at that moment. From memory, she recited the ancient words: "The Lord is my shepherd," she began. She could still sense "the shadow of death" in the room.

Sarah studied the daguerreotype. The dead Rebel soldier was wearing a clean, pressed gray uniform and standing behind a pretty woman seated in a chair. Tom had aged since this picture was taken, and Sarah marveled at the effects the last years had taken on the soldier. She guessed that the man whose body was now in her parlor was barely thirty, younger than her John. The photographic process had not captured the light golden streaks in his brown hair. They were evident now as the morning light shone through the parlor's windows. No one ever smiled in pictures. So, of course, the man and woman held their lips straight, but the camera still caught something in Tom's eyes that implied they often twinkled with laughter.

The blonde woman seated beside him was smaller-boned than her husband. Small-boned, Sarah again thought to herself, not weak. Her dress was probably her Sunday best, but even so, it spoke of respectability, not elegance. Sarah thought that if she could examine the dress closely, she would see neat handmade stitches.

Sarah turned the image over and saw the names that she knew would be written there: Mattie and Tom, first anniversary, May 22, 1861. She imagined that Mattie and Tom posed for the picture right before he left home.

She then opened the pouch and found two letters, the first of which was signed, Your loving wife, Mattie. She wrote to tell him joyous news. She and Tom were going to have the baby they had always wanted. The other letter was from his brother's wife. You could still see where Tom's tears had landed on the paper. Mattie had died in childbirth. His brother's family had taken his son to raise.

It was then that Sarah's tears came. She could not stop them. First, she cried for Tom and Mattie, but soon the tears changed and she was weeping inconsolably. The death of Tom, her enemy, triggered the tears that she had suppressed since she received the letter about John's death. She felt a gentle presence in the room. At that moment, she did not try to understand it, but she knew it was Tom's spirit. In allowing herself to actually feel the pain, Sarah began to move away from the empty feelings that had enveloped her for the last two years. Tom's spirit sat beside her as she cried. Tom understood her tears. He had shed his own for his beloved Mattie. The spirit and she shared a bond. It was the bond of two people who grieved someone they loved. Sarah knew Tom was there to send her a message. He was there to tell her that death was not the end. If his spirit lived on, then so did John's. She no longer felt alone.

It was in that moment that Tom found a home in the Calafont house. As Sarah's tears flowed, he realized that he still had a purpose. He could offer Sarah comfort. There was nothing drawing his spirit back to North Carolina with Mattie gone. Without a proper closure to his own life, he was unable to move to the afterlife. So, his spirit stayed in the old limestone house.

Four

Matthew Calafont never doubted that Tom's spirit remained in his home. He knew.

Matthew was thirteen the night Tom died. He marked that night as one of the turning points in his life. He watched his mother cry, and when her tears ceased, she had emerged anew. The next day, she had asked him to dig a grave for the soldier. He and his mother stood quietly as they laid Tom's body in the shallow grave. He then made a cross from a piece of wood and carved the name Tom on it and the date, June 29, 1863. His mother started to pray, "Our Father, who art in heaven," and Matthew recited the words with her. After the prayer, he and his

mother stood quietly for a moment. He reached out and took her hand, and together they walked back into the limestone house.

From that moment forward, Matthew forged a new relationship with his mother. He was no longer her little boy. Matthew Calafont was becoming a man.

The hard shell that Sarah had built to protect herself cracked. Her eyes no longer looked so sad. She let go of her own anger. Instead of wrapping herself around her loss, she opened up to others. In allowing herself to be comforted, she was able to comfort others. Sarah Calafont was among the first to visit a family after a death, bringing with her a baked good from her kitchen. When she felt lonely, she sat in the parlor where Tom died. She felt the comforting presence of Tom's spirit and knew that she was never truly alone.

Matthew knew that his mother often sat in the parlor at night, and more than once he saw Tom's spirit in his material form sitting beside her.

Tom's spirit never scared Matthew. With his father gone, there were no men in the house. The spirit helped to fill this vacuum. There was no doubt that Tom had been a man. He was very masculine and always appeared dressed in his military uniform. However, the spirit showed Matthew that strength did not always equate to violence. Instead, Tom's spirit gave off an aura of calm and stability.

Sarah Calafont was proud of the man her son became. He was a good man, widely respected by others. When Matthew Calafont gave his word, he kept it. His handshake was as good as his signature on a contract.

The mother and son openly acknowledged that Tom's spirit lived in the Calafont house. Soon the story of the Calafont ghost was part of the community lore. And if Matthew Calafont claimed that his house was haunted, it was good enough for most.

Mathew felt it was his duty to watch over his mother. Perhaps it was his devotion to her that kept him from finding his own soulmate sooner. He was almost thirty-seven when he met Rachel. She lived on a neighboring farm. They fit together well. After they wed, Matthew brought her home to the Calafont house to live.

Sarah welcomed her new daughter-in-law. The two women honored the traditions of the earlier Calafont women by washing the windows and polishing the silver every June.

Rachel loved to sing and play piano, so Matthew bought her one for the parlor. He had it shipped all the way from the Steinway company in New York. The Calafont house was a happy place, filled with laughter and music. Rachel, whose voice was meant for the old Scottish ballads, often sang as her fingers pressed the black and white keys.

In listening to Rachel, Tom thought they sounded like the songs that Mattie sang when she kneaded bread.

He and Mattie never could have afforded the Calafont's grand piano, though.

Matthew and Rachel had almost given up the hope of having children, but in 1892, when Matthew turned forty-two, Rachel brought forth a son. They named him Robert, after Rachel's father.

Matthew tried to pass on his love of the land to his son, but Robert was not drawn to farming. From an early age, Robert Calafont showed that he was destined to be a businessman.

In 1917, the family was blessed to have three generations living under one roof. Robert followed his father's lead and brought his wife home to live in the limestone house. However, the Calafont family life was soon disrupted. Increasingly, the morning papers sounded the drumbeats for America to enter the war in Europe. Fighting had been going on for years before Woodrow Wilson sent American sons to fight. Wilson claimed that this new war would be the "war to end all wars." Robert was among those sent "over there."

Matthew took a train to Philadelphia to watch his son's regiment leave on a ship bound for the fighting. The crowd cheered loudly and a band played patriotic tunes. Matthew had a difficult time joining the cheers with any degree of enthusiasm, for he remembered that war had taken his father's life. Matthew's thoughts also went to the spirit that lived in his house. He knew that Tom had been displaced by war.

How many of these men will not come back? Matthew wondered.

People called it "the Great War," but, unfortunately, twenty-two years later, it was clear that Wilson had been wrong. The name of this war had to be changed to World War I, for another far deadlier worldwide conflict erupted.

Matthew returned to the limestone house after Robert's departure and learned that his mother was ill. He rushed to her bedside. It was not her first bad spell, but he knew that it was different this time. He reached out and took his mother's hand. Matthew sensed something new in her breathing: the end of Sarah Calafont's mortal life was near. The atmosphere in the room changed. It became calm, and a sense of peace pervaded the space. Matthew realized that Tom's spirit was in the room. Fifty-five years after Sarah Calafont comforted Tom in his last moments, his spirit was there to comfort her.

"Are you here, Tom?" Sarah called out.

The spirit moved closer and Sarah relaxed. It was her time. She closed her eyes and took her last breath.

But the cycle of life continued. Matthew knew that Anna, his daughter-in-law, was expecting a baby.

Five

The Calafont family was luckier than many. Robert came home from the war and was able to hold his baby daughter Amelia in his arms. She was born while he was still in Europe. Again, three generations of the family were living in the old limestone house.

Robert was able to put the war and fighting behind him. If the year in Europe had touched his soul, it was not apparent to those who knew him. Robert was comfortable with numbers and ledgers. Under his watchful eyes, the Calafont fortunes grew. He made conservative investments and knew the value of cash. Although many around them suffered during the hard times, the family weathered the Great Depression with minimal hardship. Robert was prepared when the stock market crashed in October of 1929, and due to the Calafont's assets in the Cumberland Mutual Trust, Robert was named as the financial institution's president.

Robert, too, accepted the fact that Tom's spirit lived in the house. When he was a boy, he saw the spirit in material form and was accustomed to curtains ruffling and furniture moving. It was a rather inconvenient truth for him. It did not fit with his logical take on the world. He was a little impatient with his father and his grandmother when they talked about Tom as if he were a real member of the family. He never developed a personal connection to the spirit or, for that matter, with most people, including his wife, Anna.

Anna was a quiet woman, a little devoid of personality. She always did her duty, which included bringing children into the world. Unfortunately, she was not able to produce a son to carry on the family name, only two daughters named Amelia and Emily.

Matthew Calafont acknowledged to himself that he never felt a strong connection to his son. They were two very different people. However, there was no question for Matthew that his son's family should reside in the family home. It was where Calafonts lived.

For Robert, it was a fiscally wise decision for his family to reside in the old house. He did not really feel an emotional attachment to his home, but since it was one of the oldest houses in the valley, it gave him a certain status in the community. Robert was a busy man and was proud that he could provide for his family. He did not really spend much time with his daughters, but in no way, could one say that he ever mistreated them.

Matthew added an additional wing to the old house so that Robert and Anna could have their own living area. The new addition included a library next to the parlor on the first floor. After his own Rachel died, Matthew spent every evening there. He would sit in front of the large fireplace and read a book into the late hours or complete the puzzles he loved. In the early evening, his granddaughters curled up at his feet and he told them stories.

Amelia, with her dark red hair, and Emily, with her brown curls, were all ears as their grandfather talked. They loved to hear of the first Calafont who came into the valley and built a home for his new bride. The two little girls learned that he carted the chest of drawers with the pretty legs all the way from Philadelphia to give to their great-great-grandmother as a wedding present.

Matthew told his granddaughters of his own father who had died at the First Battle of Manassas helping to save the Union.

Then, Matthew Calafont pulled out the picture of Tom and Mattie. He told the two wide-eyed little girls about the night Tom's spirit came to live in the house. (The spirit hovered close by and listened.) As Matthew told of his mother opening his knapsack and finding the daguerreotype, Tom's spirit rustled the curtains.

"See, Amelia and Emily," Matthew said, "Tom is listening right now. He will always be here to watch over you, just as I watch over you."

Six

As the years passed, Tom's North Carolina world faded to the background. He considered the Calafont family "his family." He watched their comings and goings with great interest. The family members grew older, but Tom's spirit did not change. He stayed the same.

There were benefits to being a spirit. Without a mortal body, Tom no longer suffered pain; however, the fact that he understood pain gave him special empathetic gifts. As he did with Sarah, he was able to comfort those suffering.

The Calafont family felt Tom's gentle presence. In a way the adults could not really define, he offered support. Tom's spirit was by their side when they were depressed. He absorbed their emotions and, consequently, lessened some of their intensity. His spirit helped to bring a sense of calm to the old house in times of trouble.

Tom struggled with the limitations of being a spirit. He could not speak or really interact on a human level with the people in the big limestone house. The popular mortal conception was that spirits could float through walls or other physical barriers. Perhaps, other spirits had that capability, but Tom did not. When his spirit bumped into a physical item, he bounced off it, often causing it to move in the process. He soon developed a method of moving objects to make his presence known. He was able to materialize, but it took a lot of energy. He found that he was very tired afterwards, and the longer he remained a spirit, the harder it became for him to appear to humans. When Tom did materialize, he looked as if he had stepped right out of the picture found in his knapsack: a Confederate soldier, dressed in a clean, pressed, gray uniform; he did not look like the suffering soldier in dirty ragtag clothing who died in the Calafont parlor.

Amelia and Emily, Matthew's granddaughters, captured Tom's heart. They were special. He was at their births, four years apart, in one of the upstairs bedrooms. When they were very little, he was their imaginary friend who entertained them by materializing as part of their games. Tom was their guest at their tea parties. The girls' ritual was always the same:

Amelia, the older sister, mimicked her mother's actions. She picked up the child's teapot and graciously pretended to pour tea in the cups.

"Now, Emily, you must gently pick up the teacup and sip the tea," Amelia instructed her younger sister.

"Like this, Amelia?" Emily asked.

"Almost, Emily," Amelia always answered.

Again, Amelia would be the grand lady with her tea-cup, showing the younger sister how to hold it. It was part of the game.

"I think Tom needs a cup, too. Don't you, Amelia?" Emily always said.

Amelia agreed and pretended to pour another cup of tea.

Tom knew that was his cue to appear, and he obliged the girls.

Emily could not resist clapping but Amelia was more dignified. She tried to sound as grown up as her mother, and said, "Welcome Tom. This is a special blend of tea all the way from India. I trust that you will like it."

Anna and Robert were a little concerned about these games. Robert especially was uncomfortable with the spirit as his daughters' playmate. They openly worried about the situation at dinner one night. Matthew, the family patriarch, entered into the discussion.

"We are very lucky that Tom's spirit found a home in our house. He helped my mother through the worst days of her life. His presence changed our house. He came to us as a man engaged in war, but he brought my mother peace. I can think of no better playmate for my grand-daughters than Tom's spirit."

Anna and Robert never again complained about the spirit in Matthew's presence.

Seven

The girls grew older and the tea parties became a thing of the past. Tom no longer materialized to entertain the girls. Without making his presence known, he watched their activities from his perch on top of the mantel. Amelia had inherited her grandmother Rachel's musical ability. She played Rachel's beautiful piano, filling the limestone house with music most afternoons. Like her grandmother, she often sang as she played. Tom's spirit loved to listen to her. He knew how she was feeling by the music she played.

The limestone house became a gathering place for Amelia and Emily's friends. Although the country was in the middle of the Great Depression, the hard times did not keep the girls from having fun. There were always young people in the house, especially boys who courted the two Calafont girls. They would gather around to sing as Amelia played the piano, or the boys would roll up the rugs in the parlor so they could dance. Tom loved watching the fun.

All too soon for Tom's liking, Amelia and Emily left home for college. First, Amelia left for Bryn Mawr, and then a few years later, Emily followed in her footsteps. None of the Calafont women had previously received a college degree, but Robert's hard work gave his daughters new opportunities. If the world would not have exploded, both girls probably would have graduated and then waited for the right man to come along to marry. That man may have joined one of Robert's business enterprises, and life in the limestone house would have continued in a predictable way. However, the world did explode.

On a Sunday morning in early December of 1941, the Japanese bombed Pearl Harbor. Life for Amelia and Emily, along with everyone in America, took a new direction. The prescribed planned world for the two Calafont girls did not happen. Emily never lived in the limestone house again after college; she came home for a week in December of 1945 for her wedding. World War II was over, and Emily was just one of thousands of American women who were married that month.

Tom watched Emily float down the large staircase in her wedding dress to marry the good-looking young pilot dressed in his Army Air Corps uniform. Her pretty brown curls were tucked underneath her veil. It was such a special day, and Tom never forgot the joy on Emily's face. Her glow reminded him of Mattie's face the day they were married.

Soon after their wedding, Emily and her new husband left the Calafont house to make their home in the Midwest.

Life took a different turn for Amelia. Her World War II love story did not end at the altar. The love of her life was killed in the last days of fighting in Europe. She came home to the limestone house to stay. She filled her days with teaching the young children in the area.

Tom noticed that Amelia's sparkling eyes carried a sadness with her that he understood. He tried to comfort her, just as he had once comforted her great-grandmother, Sarah.

Amelia missed Emily, and so she kept in touch with her sister by writing letters. But, sadly, like Mattie, her sister's story ended too soon. She stopped receiving Emily's letters after a phone call in 1953.

Tom watched Amelia's face turn pale as she talked on the phone that day. He heard the word "polio." Emily had been taken by the dreaded disease. Tom knew enough to understand that polio was an indiscriminate killer. No one yet understood why some people were stricken and others spared. The vaccine to prevent it was still a few years away. Together, Tom and Amelia grieved Emily's death. Tom listened to Amelia play Chopin's Prelude in E Minor that spring. It sounded so sad to him.

Robert and Anna died of old age during the 1960s, leaving Amelia the only Calafont left in the old house.

For the last fifty years, Tom's spirit and Amelia kept each other company. Until her arthritis got the best of her, Tom listened to her play the piano most nights. When

Miss Amelia's voice sounded especially fine, he could not help but ruffle the lace curtains to show his appreciation.

"Oh, you like that one, did you, Tom?" Miss Amelia would say.

Music, laughter, and tears are the sounds of life. The Calafont house always had those sounds in abundance. There was always noise inside the limestone walls. The old house no longer carried the sounds of the living. Sarah, Matthew, Robert, and now Amelia were all gone, leaving Tom all alone and no longer needed. The old house was absolutely quiet.

Quiet as a tomb, Tom thought.

Tom did not like living in a tomb. He felt hopeless.

PART

II

Eight

Washington, D.C.

March 23, 2011

The law offices of Hamilton, Hamilton, and Blakely took up the top three floors of a large office building on Connecticut Avenue, just a few blocks from the White House. People in the know in the nation's capital called the firm H. H. & B. Its partners had important connections in the political world, but the prestigious firm was also known for its first-rate advice in real estate matters, estate planning, and trusts.

On a Wednesday morning, in the final days of March of 2011, an associate of the firm, Bob McPherson, opened the thick Calafont file folder on his desk. It was the first time Bob looked at the Calafont file. The Calafont legal issues had always been handled by the firm's managing partner, Mark Hamilton. Yesterday, that changed. Mark Hamilton asked Bob to personally handle the estate of Miss Amelia Calafont.

Lately, Bob noticed that Mark was turning over more and more clients to him. He knew that the firm's senior partner was lessening his workload since he and his wife wanted to spend their winters in Florida. Bob joined the firm ten years earlier, right out of Georgetown Law School, and Hamilton had taken a special interest in him almost from the start. His interest seemed almost paternal at times.

Everyone in the firm knew that Bob was on his way to becoming the next head of Hamilton, Hamilton, and Blakely's trust department and obviously in line to be a partner in the firm.

Bob was surprised at his mentor's words on Tuesday. His pending retirement seemed to bring out Mark's sentimental side, a side that Bob had seldom seen.

"Bob," Mark said, "H.H. & B. has handled Calafont legal affairs since my great-grandfather started the firm. Amelia Calafont originally named my father as the executor of her estate when he drafted her will. After he died, she transferred that responsibility to me. I know you think it a little strange that I would take such an interest in an estate matter, but the Calafont house holds strong memories for me. My father took me to visit Miss Amelia when I was a boy. I never forgot it. She gave me the best ginger cookies.

"I know that we will probably end up arranging to sell the house and land. A bothersome developer has tried to buy it from Miss Amelia for years. The house will probably be torn down and replaced with the standard boxes that are cropping up on what was once farmland. It makes me sad to see that fate for the Calafont house."

Bob had never heard Mark Hamilton, friend to politicians and judges, express emotions when it came to a case or a client. For Hamilton, it was always about the facts and the law. It was clear that the Calafont family was no ordinary client for Mark Hamilton. Without saying it directly, Bob knew that his mentor expected him to clear his desk and make the Calafont estate his priority. Bob did not say a word as Mark continued.

"It was Amelia's desire to leave all her worldly possessions to the descendants of her sister Emily," Mark said, however, the last correspondence she had with her sister's family was in the late 1950s. Emily died very young, leaving behind a husband and a small son. Amelia corresponded for a while with her brother-in-law, but lost track of him after he remarried and relocated. I need you to find Emily's son if he is still alive, or if not, find his descendants.

"Clear your calendar in the next couple of weeks and let's drive to the Cumberland Valley. As the executor of the estate, I need to access its condition and determine the value of the property. Also, you will need to arrange to have the contents of the house appraised. Besides, there are likely clues regarding Emily's family in the old place. I must admit I look forward to seeing the Calafont house again."

The thick file folder was divided into sections. Bob pulled out one marked donations and gifts. There was a record of cashier checks made out to various charities and individuals apparently down on their luck. They totaled a sizeable amount of money. Bob realized that Mark had handled them in such a way that the recipients had no idea that the money came from Amelia Calafont. When Bob opened the next file folder, he whistled softly. He realized that these donations, while sizable, did not make a dent in Amelia's estate.

Amelia Calafont's assets went way beyond land in Central Pennsylvania. Her stock holdings were impressive, easily worth over five or six million dollars. Apparently, she had gotten in on the ground floor of some of the best tech and pharmaceutical investment opportunities. Her portfolio was handled by a Washington brokerage firm with Al Baker listed as her financial agent.

Small world, Bob thought.

Al played on Bob's softball team. Bob picked up his phone. It would not hurt to find out as much as possible about Amelia Calafont.

"Good game last Friday night," Bob said when Al picked up the phone.

"It's always a good game when you win," Al replied. He waited to find out what Bob really wanted.

Al did not have to wait long, as Bob got right to the point of his call.

"We are handling the estate of one of your former clients who just passed away. I thought you might be able to give me some information about her," Bob said.

"Sure, I'll try, if the information is not confidential. Who's the client?" Al replied.

"Amelia Calafont," Bob said.

Without needing to check his computer or files, Al said, "Oh, I will miss her. She was my favorite and easiest client. She called me frequently to give me her instructions. She made all her own stock picks. Let me tell you, I have never worked with anyone who was as good at it as she was. She had an uncanny ability to identify trends and patterns. She knew when to sell and when to buy. When I had any extra money, I followed her investment advice. I never regretted it. She missed her calling. Instead of being a school teacher, she should have been a hedge fund manager."

After some more small talk, Bob hung up the phone. He was becoming very curious about Amelia Calafont. Obviously, there was more to her than met the eye.

Nine

Bob rose early on a Monday a few weeks after his call with Al. He and Mark were scheduled to drive to the Calafont house, and he wanted to go for a run in Rock Creek Park before he had to sit in a car all day.

Bob hated days that did not allow him time to exercise. At thirty-five, his body was still fit. He had run track during his undergraduate days at Carleton College. In addition to being a shortstop on his softball team, he regularly played racquetball with a law school classmate. Last year, he and Lisa, his girlfriend, broke up. She called him a workaholic when she ended their year and a half relationship. By keeping up with his sports routine, he felt that he was proving her wrong.

"See," he told himself, "I am not just a lawyer," but in reality, more and more of his time seemed to be spent at his office.

It was a beautiful spring day, but Bob didn't even notice the budding flowers as he ran beside the creek. Instead, he was thinking of the Calafont estate. Last week he had studied the papers in the file in detail. They went back centuries, some even before the American Revolution. He knew that Amelia was the last Calafont to reside in the house. She was born there in an upstairs bedroom in 1918 and died in the house six months ago, in 2010. He marveled at the changes in the world during her lifetime. He had formed a picture in his mind of the house and wondered how accurate it was.

Bob was breathing a little heavily after his five-mile run when he unlocked the door to his condo. He quickly jumped into the shower, and afterwards looked closely at himself in the mirror after he shaved. He never felt he was suited for facial hair and always felt scraggly if he didn't shave his light beard every day. He examined his full head of brown hair; at least he didn't appear to be losing any of it. He selected a conservative blue tie and finished dressing. He needed to get a move on if he was going to meet Mark Hamilton on time.

It made sense for Bob to drive to Mark's Leesburg, Virginia, home and leave his car there. Mark loved driving his new convertible BMW, and Bob was more than happy to give him an opportunity to do so.

Jackie Hamilton teased her husband, that at sixty-five, he was going through his second mid-life crisis.

Bob knew his manager's wife well. Bob visited the Hamilton home often and Mark's wife had taken a special, almost maternal, interest in him.

Jackie Hamilton looked young for her fifty-nine years. She ran a successful home decorating business, and her house reflected her unique style. Their home was in the Virginia horse country, and she was what one would describe as a *horsewoman*. She pampered her horses as if they were her grandbabies. She was open about it and said that as a grandmother, she had to have something to baby. Jackie jokingly complained that her daughter kept her from enjoying her life by choosing to keep her children from her by living in California with her son-in-law, an executive in Silicon Valley.

To be honest, Bob did not know anyone who enjoyed life more than Jackie. She had a light informal touch that was a nice counterbalance to Mark's professional drive. Bob adored her. She worried about him and often invited him for dinner. When he had a bad case of the flu this last year, Jackie personally brought him homemade chicken noodle soup. She sat with him for hours, spooning the soup into his mouth, and watched over him until she was sure that he would keep the soup down. He wished that she did not take her mission of finding him a wife so seriously, though, because from the moment that his girlfriend, Lisa, was no longer in the picture, she had made a point of introducing him to every eligible woman she knew.

About an hour after leaving D.C., Bob turned down the long driveway to the Hamilton home. Stately oaks lined the driveway. The tulip beds were blooming and the whole scene looked like a cover of *House and Garden*. He knocked on the door and Jackie answered.

"It is so good to see you," Jackie said, giving Bob a big hug. "It's been a couple of months since you were here for dinner."

It did not take long for Jackie to bring up her most recent candidate for Bob's affection.

"Did you have a chance to call Abigail Moore?"

Jackie couldn't help herself. She was a born matchmaker.

"You know I didn't feel any sparks when I met her at your last dinner party," Bob said. "I think you need to keep trying. I don't think Abigail is going to be *the one*!

"Well, it was always clear to me that Lisa was not right for you," Jackie said, giving him an affectionate pat on the cheek. "You know I want only the best for you. You deserve it."

Bob was happy that she chose to change the topic.

"Seriously, I need you to watch over Mark today. I do not want the two of you to just casually wander down to Gettysburg. I am planning a loin roast for dinner tonight. You will stay for dinner, won't you? If Mark gets lost in the Civil War, the roast will be dry. He will try to tell you that you can just make a quick stop in order for him to explain some intricate detail regarding troop movements on the second day of the battle, but let me tell you, Mark is incapable of a *quick* trip to the Gettysburg Battlefield. Last July, he made me walk Pickett's Charge with him. If he would have let me ride a horse like Jeb Stuart, I might have enjoyed it more."

Mark laughed as he entered the room. He had over-heard his wife's words. "Jackie, you will never get your commanders straight. Jeb Stuart wasn't at Pickett's Charge. Now, don't worry, Bob and I are on a business trip today. There are enough war stories around the Calafont house to keep us entertained. We should be back in plenty of time to have cocktails before I have to carve your roast. But if we are going to do so, we need to get started."

Mark gave his wife an affectionate kiss goodbye.

Bob felt a sense of being alone. He envied their close relationship. Last year, Mark and Jackie celebrated their thirtieth wedding anniversary. Bob had a feeling that the years were slipping by and he was missing out on something important.

Ten

While driving through the Virginia countryside to Interstate 81 in Winchester, Bob brought up Mark's favorite subject, the American Civil War.

"This area saw a lot of action during the war, didn't it?" Bob asked, somewhat rhetorically.

He did not bother to identify *which* war. He knew that for Mark, one war mattered above all others.

It was fair to call Mark Hamilton a Civil War buff. In his office, the firm's senior partner had several Civil War prints on the wall as well as blue and gray miniature soldiers in a curio cabinet in the corner. Bob was interested in history, but he did not share Mark's passion for the subject.

"Yes," Mark said, "Ewell, one of Robert E. Lee's three major commanders, took Winchester right before his troops marched north to fight in the campaign that culminated in the Battle of Gettysburg. Lee divided his troops into three corps that all came together again in Pennsylvania."

Interested in spite of himself, Bob listened as Mark told of the Confederates' movements.

"Ewell's corps headed north, first with the intent of taking Harrisburg. Instead, they were pulled back from the Pennsylvania capital by a message from Lee that the Army of the Potomac had followed the Confederates into Pennsylvania and were gathering to the south in Adams County."

As they drove over South Mountain and entered the Cumberland Valley around Chambersburg, Mark continued with his tale of the Southern soldiers who had marched from Northern Virginia over the mountains into Pennsylvania.

"Those soldiers moved quickly. One writer said that on the same day, 'they had breakfast in Virginia, drank whiskey in Maryland, and ate hardtack for supper in Pennsylvania.' Ewell's troops spread over this area. As a matter of fact, Rebel troops marched in front of the old Calafont home."

"It is pretty country, isn't it?" Bob said. "It's hard to imagine troops marching through it."

"There is a letter that a Confederate soldier sent his wife just before the big battle," Mark said. "He wrote her that Pennsylvania was some of the prettiest land he ever saw."

The valley was bordered by two mountain ranges, to the south was South Mountain and to the north, Blue Mountain. The mountain ranges gave Bob a protected feeling. He saw the sign announcing that they had entered Cumberland County, the location of the Calafont home. They turned off the main interstate and drove down a road known locally as Walnut Bottom.

Mark was on a roll now, talking about the Confederate soldiers who marched down this road almost a century and a half earlier.

"In 1863, this was a dirt road with deep ruts. It was used frequently, since the neighboring road was a toll road. I'm always struck by the fact that many of the Southern soldiers who passed this way had only a few days left to live."

Bob had a difficult time thinking about war when he looked at the peaceful bucolic scenery. He tried to put his head around the idea of tens of thousands of soldiers dying at Gettysburg. His ears perked up and he listened more closely when Mark mentioned their client's land.

"See these houses to our left. They sit on what was originally Calafont land," Mark said.

Bob looked at the modern large homes. He knew that housing prices were much less here than in the Washington, D.C. area, but even in Central Pennsylvania, these homes spoke of affluence. He knew from the papers in the Calafont file folder that Amelia's father had sold the land in the early 1960s. The sale of the land must have given Amelia money to use for her investments. *It always takes money to make money*, he thought as Mark returned to his favorite subject.

"You know my interest in the Civil War really started when I visited Amelia Calafont as a boy. Her house looked much the same then as it did when the Confederate troops marched across Calafont land. You appreciate the foot soldier in this part of the country. I always thought that the reason so many of them died of disease was that their bodies were just worn out. They just *'gave up the ghost'*, or if you believe in the many legends around this area, the ghost stayed behind. I told you, didn't I, that the Calafont house is haunted by a Confederate soldier?" Mark mused.

Bob found Mark's choice of words startling. Mark Hamilton, always reasoned and clear headed, now used the word *haunted* as if it were a fact, not just an interesting old tale. Bob could not help but respond to his boss with surprise.

"Come on, Mark, you of all people do not really believe in ghosts, do you?" Bob said.

"The Calafont house may make you question your sense of reality. Remember your Shakespeare? Hamlet was very wise," Mark said, quoting a famous line from the play: 'There are more things in heaven and earth, Horatio, than are dreamt of in your philosophy.'"

Eleven

The Limestone House

April 11, 2011

Tom's spirit heard the car come up the driveway. He quickly flew to the window so he could see who was disturbing his world. Two men got out of the car and headed to the house. They were strangers to him. The older man was probably in his middle sixties, a little overweight, but clearly a person of substance. The younger man conveyed deference to the older man as he listened to him talk.

Neither Bob nor Mark were aware that they were being watched. Bob noticed that there were a few minor repairs that needed to be done to the outside of the house. He made a note about them on a yellow legal pad that he carried; however, he was a pleasantly surprised that the house was in remarkably good shape, given its age.

Tom was alarmed when the older man pulled out a key to unlock the front door and the two men entered the house.

Once inside, Bob looked around. The house had clearly been lived in by people who cared about it.

"That's strange," Bob said, looking at the window.

The window was definitely closed, but he noticed that the lace curtains flared out as if they were caught by a breeze. He moved into the room that he assumed was once called the parlor. He knew very little about antiques, but it did not require an expert to see that the furniture was from an earlier era.

"It looks to me as if there are some valuable pieces here," Bob said as he began to make notes on his pad about the furniture.

"Yes," Mark said. "In its day, the Calafont home was one of the showplaces of the valley. My father attended parties here before World War II, and, then, during the war, he and Amelia Calafont were friends. My father was a naval officer before he went to law school. Amelia worked in D.C., doing something for the war effort. My dad never said what she actually did during the war, but I know they traveled in the same circles."

"I wonder why she never married?" Bob asked rhetorically.

"I always wondered about that myself. From what my father said, she was an unusual beauty, with striking auburn hair. I always thought that as much as my father loved my mother, Amelia Calafont held a special place in his heart. But Amelia never returned his feelings. She returned to this house after the war and my dad went to law school and joined the family firm. The rest is history. He became the second Hamilton of Hamilton, Hamilton, and Blakely and married my mother a few years later."

Bob moved into the pristine room that Mamie Hodges had cleaned on her visit to the house the previous day. There was not a speck of dust to be seen; however, the house felt unoccupied. It was interesting how quickly a house could feel that way. The room had high ceilings and a large wood burning fire place. Above the mantel was an oil painting of two young girls, the younger one with brown curls and the older one with pretty auburn hair. As he moved closer to the fireplace, he felt a strange chill. Bob had an uncomfortable feeling that he was being watched. He almost shivered. The curtains again flared out. He made another note on his paper to consider having the structure of the house examined. There seemed to be a draft in the room.

Mark was lost in his own thoughts. In his memory, he was again the thirteen-year-old boy who visited this house with his father. It was the year 1966. Bill Hamilton was the executor of Robert Calafont's will and wanted to personally deliver some business papers to Amelia Calafont. Thinking back, Mark thought that his father probably wanted an excuse to see Amelia again. It was a special day for Mark. His father was always busy, but that day he had included Mark in his world. He felt very grown up to be spending a work day with his father.

On that day, almost half a century earlier, Mark became bored with the adult conversation between Amelia and his father. He took several of the ginger cookies Miss Amelia offered him and wandered into the parlor. He was standing about where Bob was now when he saw Tom. The spirit was standing with his hand on the mantle, dressed in the gray of a Confederate uniform. The solider smiled at him and then held his finger up to his lips, indicating that Mark should not say anything. In just a few minutes, the spirit disappeared, but Mark knew he was not imagining what he had seen.

Mark drew himself back to the present and watched Bob walk toward the baby grand piano that dominated the room. It was a beautiful instrument.

Bob knew that the Steinway name meant something in music circles. He played a quick scale.

Tom's spirit was incensed. *How dare that stranger touch Miss Amelia's piano!*

The spirit reached out and closed the lid, protecting the keys with a bang.

Bob was playing before the lid suddenly came down and he barely managed to get his hands out of the way.

Tom quickly moved backwards and bumped into the piano. In the process, one of the framed photographs sitting on the piano fell down.

Startled by what had just happened, Bob picked up the photo that fell to the floor. It was a picture of a pretty woman with curly brown hair, holding a baby on her lap. Bob turned the photograph over and read the inscription out loud: "Emily Calafont Monroe with Matthew, age six months, Kansas City, Kansas, 1947." Bob thought for a moment, and then said, "I guess Matthew would be in his middle sixties now."

"He is the man you must locate," Mark said.

Bob tucked the photo into his folder.

The men walked around the large house. It spoke of a bygone era. The parlor was separated from a formal dining room by heavy walnut sliding doors that fit into the pocket made for them in the wall. The dining room had crown molding and contained two fine pieces of furniture, a china cabinet and a breakfront. The china cabinet held china collected by several generations of Calafont women. The seats of the dining room chairs were covered in intricate needlepoint designs.

Bob continued making notes on his legal pad as they went from room to room.

The library, which was on the other side of the parlor, had floor–to–ceiling bookcases and a substantive walnut desk with a large chair behind it. In front of the desk were two additional leather chairs that looked surprisingly comfortable.

As Bob entered the library, he noticed the bookcases first. He loved books, so he examined the titles of some of the volumes. He wondered if any were first editions. He made another note on the pad to contact a rare book appraiser about the books in the library.

The kitchen was in the back of the house. It had been remodeled, probably in the 1970s, so while the appliances were a little dated, they were still serviceable. It was a large room with a table in the center of it. A comfortable sunroom had been added behind the kitchen. It was obviously an addition, but it had been designed with the original house in mind. You could sit in the room and see South Mountain in the distance. In the adjacent yard were rose bushes, although it was too early for them to have buds.

Continuing their tour of the old house, Bob and Mark headed back to the entryway and started up the wide staircase to the second floor.

Bob's hand glided over the shiny banister that Mamie Hodges had polished the previous day.

As the two men looked into the five bedrooms on the second floor, Bob noticed the bedroom furniture. His eyes were drawn to the chest of drawers in one of the bedrooms. The delicate legs were carved and the drawer handles were made of brass. He remembered the expression "Philadelphia style" and thought that might be the term for this piece. Many of his friends had such furniture in their bedrooms, but he knew they were reproductions. He thought the chest in the Calafont bedroom might be an original, so he made another note on his yellow pad.

Seeing a short staircase at the end of the hallway, Bob said, "Those stairs must go to an attic and the dormer windows that we can see from the outside. I wonder what's stored up there?"

Despite his curiosity, Bob made no move to go up those stairs. Attics can be creepy places, even in houses that do not reputedly have a resident ghost.

Bob and Mark headed down the long Calafont driveway as they set out for Virginia. Bob took notice of the tulips blooming along the sidewalk as well as the first buds on the trees. While he was inside the house, he had forgotten what a beautiful April day it was, and it made him think of another quote from the bard: "… The uncertain glory of an April day …", from *Two Gentleman from Verona*, which he had read in a college literature class.

What surprised Bob most about the day was that Mark accepted with more than a degree of certainty that the spirit of a Confederate soldier resided in the old house. Bob was certainly unnerved by the Calafont house, as he had definitely felt a chill in the room by the old fireplace, and he did not imagine that the curtains flared and the piano lid closed all by itself for no discernible reason. He just couldn't buy the idea of a ghost living in the house. He had no answer to the events that he just experienced, but there must be a logical answer. But unlike his boss, Bob was not certain about anything at that point in time.

Twelve

Lawrence, Kansas

May 27, 2011

Callie Anne Monroe was lying face up on the grass in her back yard. Lawrence, Kansas, was in the middle of an early heat wave. It was the Friday afternoon before the Memorial Day weekend, and although it was barely 11 a.m., the thermometer already registered eighty-five degrees. The temperature said summer, but Callie still had one more week of school before the year ended.

Classes had been dismissed early, since the teachers were busy finishing up the paperwork required by state law. In Callie's mind, the school year was already over. She knew that nothing would happen next week. She and her best friend, Brenna, had wrapped up their science project a couple of weeks ago, and today she turned in her last required composition. She knew she would receive a good grade on it—she always made good grades. Callie knew what was expected of her and she always met those expectations, sometimes without trying. Middle school was almost a thing of the past. She and Brenna were headed to high school next year.

Callie turned over and cupped her chin in her hands. Thoughts of the next year bumped into each other disjointedly in her head. She and Brenna had been tight friends since third grade. They were always in the same classes and played on the same teams. Would it be the same in high school? Would everything be different in September? Lately, she and Brenna were growing apart. Callie was bored with Brenna's constant discussions about clothes and boys. It was a challenge to work with her on their science project, as Brenna seemed more than willing to let Callie do the majority of the work. When Callie complained, Brenna lashed out at her, saying, "Oh, honestly, Callie, do you always have to be such a nerd? Do you have to take everything so seriously?"

Callie realized that Brenna was spending more of her time with the popular girls in the class. It just reinforced her feelings that her world was coming apart. She did not know if she had changed or if Brenna was different. She just knew that her world was not the same.

A lock of her dark red hair fell over Callie's eyes. She pushed it back. Her hair seemed to have a mind of its own in this heat and humidity. She thought again that it was so unfair that she looked different than everyone in her family. Her pretty mother wore her straight blonde hair in a cute short cut that framed her head. Her father's hair had been dark brown. Her red hair had been a surprise to all when she was born.

She tried to push away the sadness that she always felt when she thought about her father. He and her grandfather died two years ago when their small Cessna went down, killing both men instantly. Her grandfather had been flying the plane, but it could easily have been her father in the pilot's seat. Both her father and her Grandpa Matt had their pilot's license. She recalled her Grandpa Matt often saying, "Flying above the clouds is in the Monroe blood. We are born with invisible wings. You know my father flew missions over Germany during World War II."

The two men were in the air that day to check on the extent of flooding in Eastern Kansas. Melting snows in the Dakotas were pushing waters southward. Already the Missouri River was out of its banks north of Kansas City. Kansans were concerned that the flooding would extend across the river, into their state. Grandpa Matt was a meteorologist for the Kansas Department of Emergency Preparedness. It was part of his job to watch for rising waters. Callie's father had just gone along to keep his father company. He loved to look at the land.

"There is nothing prettier than the Kansas prairie when you look down on it from a blue sky," Callie's father often proclaimed.

No one could really explain what caused the small plane to crash. Callie no longer wanted to think about the details. She just knew that both her father and grandfather were gone.

Her school counselor told her that it would take time for the sharp pain to go away. She did feel a little better now than last year. She was able to remember the good times without feeling like she was going to cry. Her mom also seemed to be getting better. Just this morning, they laughed together over a cartoon in the newspaper. It was good to see her mother smile. She worked so hard and often seemed worried. Money was much tighter than it was before her father died. It was not that her father had made a lot of money as a professor of aeronautical engineering at the University of Kansas, but they had been comfortable. Callie knew that even with the insurance money, it was hard for her mother to stay ahead of the bills. Callie's mother loved her job as a children's librarian at the public library, but her paycheck did not seem to go far enough each month.

Callie pushed herself up off the ground. On Friday nights, it was her responsibility to start dinner, since her mother worked late at the library. She stood up and headed into the house to put the chicken in the oven. She picked up the mail that had fallen through the mail-drop in the front door and casually looked at it. She did not expect anything to be addressed to her. No one she knew ever wrote letters. Texting was their preferred

method of communicating. There were, as usual, a few bills. Callie laid them aside for her mother. The envelope addressed to her mother from Hamilton, Hamilton, and Blakely, caught her eye. It was apparently from a firm in Washington, D.C. Callie had never heard her mother mention knowing anyone in the D.C. area. It was probably some sort of advertisement or a plea for a contribution. She put the mail on the table and turned to the refrigerator to begin dinner preparations.

Thirteen

Lee Anne Monroe looked tired when she walked through the door of their modest split-level home. She had spent much of the day on her feet at the check-out desk of the library. She was exhausted. The smell of the chicken baking in the oven greeted her. Again, she thought how proud she was of Callie. Her daughter had really pitched in this last year. Since Lee Anne's parents were also gone, she and Callie were all alone in the world. She worried that Callie was perhaps becoming just a little too serious, but she pushed those thoughts out of her head. Right now, she needed to lean on her daughter's shoulder.

"Callie, it smells good in here," Lee Anne said, announcing she was home.

"Dinner should be ready in about fifteen minutes," Callie said.

"Perfect timing. It will give me a chance to change clothes and get out of these shoes. I am exhausted and hot. What is there about unexpected heat that makes everyone so unpleasant?" Lee Anne asked.

She picked up the mail but put it aside. There would be plenty of time to look at the bills later. It was a good decision. She was able to enjoy Callie's delicious chicken before she was faced with the large property tax bill and her quarterly car insurance payment. Together, the two bills would come close to depleting their meager savings account.

After dinner, Lee Anne picked up the envelope from Hamilton, Hamilton, and Blakely, assuming that it was some sort of promotional piece. She read the letter quickly and then sat up straight.

"Callie, come here and listen," she said, trying to keep the excitement out of her voice. She read the letter aloud.

Dear Mrs. Monroe,

Our firm represents the estate of the late Amelia Stuart Calafont of Cumberland County, Pennsylvania. After extensive research, we believe that your daughter, Callie Anne Monroe, may be a direct descendant of Miss Calafont's sister, Emily Calafont Monroe, who died in 1953. Emily Calafont Monroe appears to have been the mother of Matthew Calafont Monroe, your late husband's father.

If the relationship can be validated, Callie Anne Monroe may potentially be the beneficiary of Miss Amelia Calafont's estate.

Please contact me at your earliest convenience

"Callie, it must be a scam, but it looks real enough. What do you think?".

"I guess it wouldn't hurt to call him," Callie said.

Early Monday morning, Lee Anne and Callie placed a call to the Washington, D.C., law firm. The receptionist connected them to Mr. McPherson's office.

"Mrs. Monroe, I am so glad that you took my letter seriously. I was afraid that given the world that we live in, you would think it was a scam," Bob said after introducing himself.

"I must admit, the thought did cross my mind," Lee Anne said. "Since this matter concerns my daughter, you should be aware that she is listening in on our extension."

McPherson got right to the point. "As I explained in my letter, we represent the estate of Miss Amelia Calafont. Her will leaves a portion of her estate to the heirs of her sister, Emily Calafont Monroe. Our research shows that Emily had one son, Matthew Calafont Monroe."

"Yes, my father-in-law was named Matthew Calafont Monroe," Lee Anne said. "I know that Calafont was a family name. In fact, my husband chose Callie's name in honor of his father. I don't know anything about his mother's family. As you may know, he and my husband were both killed in a plane crash two years ago."

"I am very sorry for your loss," McPherson politely said and then continued. "Do you have any documents, such as birth certificates, that can verify that he was *the* Matthew Calafont Monroe that we are seeking? It does seem to be an unusual name."

"After Matthew and my husband were killed, we had to submit documentation in order to receive insurance benefits. I remember noticing that Matt's mother's name was Emily. I can send you copies of that material," Lee Anne said.

"That would be great. Please send it to me via certified priority mail at my firm's address. I will be back in touch as soon as we authenticate it."

Lee Anne could not help herself; she had to ask. "Would Callie's share of the estate be significant?"

"I'm not at liberty to share with you the exact amount in monetary terms," Bob said, "but I can tell you that the estate includes property and stocks. For that reason, we must validate any claims before we proceed with probating the estate. We will talk again soon, I am sure."

When they hung up, Lee Anne hugged Callie. They were both practical people—they did not want to get too excited— but it sounded like a fairy tale, and Callie had outgrown fairy tales two years ago. She learned the hard way that fairy tales do not include plane crashes.

Fourteen

Washington, D.C.

June 10, 2011

Callie and her mother flew to Washington, D.C. on June 10, 2011.

It seemed a little surreal to Lee Anne, it had all happened so fast. Mr. McPherson's associate arranged all the details.

Callie looked upon it as an adventure. She was always naturally curious. In her excitement, she lost the sense of grief that had consumed her for the last two years. Like her father and grandfather, Callie loved being above the clouds in an airplane, although this large jet was different from the small planes that her father loved. She was barely able to sit still as the plane landed at Washington's Reagan National Airport.

"It's just like the movies," Callie said to her mother when they saw a man at their gate holding a sign with the name Monroe printed on it.

The driver explained that he worked for Hamilton, Hamilton, and Blakely and that his limousine was waiting outside the door. After picking up their luggage at the baggage claim, he ushered them outside and into the humid D.C. air.

"I'm to take you directly to the firm's offices. Afterwards, I'll deliver you and your bags to the Willard Hotel in downtown D.C. Guests of the firm usually enjoy staying in the heart of D.C., in the historic hotel," he said.

"That will be fine," Lee Anne said. She felt obliged to say something, although she was feeling a little overwhelmed.

As they crossed over the Lincoln Memorial Bridge, with the memorial to the martyred president right before them, Callie turned her head and looked to their rear. She could see the eternal flame at President Kennedy's grave in Arlington Cemetery. It was a little hard for her to put her head around the fact that she was really seeing these sites in person. They looked just like the pictures in a guidebook. When the driver turned onto Constitution Avenue, Callie had a clear view of the Washington Monument and the United States Capitol. They then turned left at Connecticut Avenue, and a few blocks later pulled into a parking garage below a large modern office building on K Street. The top three floors housed the offices of Hamilton, Hamilton, and Blakely.

Callie and Lee Anne took the elevator to the top floor. When they stepped off the elevator, Lee Anne thought of the television shows she often watched. The law offices looked the way the prestigious law firms always looked on TV. Everything was decorated in rich colors of burgundy and gray, with thick wall-to-wall dark burgundy carpet on the floor. On the other side of the receptionist area was a glass-enclosed conference room.

"You must be Lee Anne and Callie Monroe," the stylish young receptionist said, greeting them cordially. "I'll ring Mr. McPherson's associate to let her know you're here."

Very shortly, another woman appeared. She was a little older and dressed in very attractive, expensive business attire. Lee Anne envied her ability to walk in her high stiletto heels, and she again felt as if she were seeing a character on a Sunday night television show.

"Hello, you must be Lee Anne, and I would guess this is Callie. I am Elizabeth Rogers ... we talked on the phone several times. I hope your flight was comfortable. Mr. Hamilton and Mr. McPherson are eager to meet you. Follow me."

Neither Lee Anne nor Callie had a chance to say anything before they were led through the opulent offices by the young lawyer. They stopped at the corner office on the top floor. The name plate on the door read Mark T. Hamilton, Managing Partner. They were led into the impressive office suite by Ms. Rogers, who then discretely made her departure.

When they entered the room, two men stood and greeted them.

"Mrs. Monroe, Callie, it's very nice to meet you. I'm Bob McPherson. We talked on the phone several times.

Let me introduce you to our firm's managing partner, Mark Hamilton."

Callie looked closely at Bob McPherson. His appearance matched his warm voice. She then turned her attention to Mark Hamilton. At first, he was a little intimidating, but she relaxed when he smiled. He had a nice smile. It was clear that he was used to being in charge. She was surprised when he addressed his next words to her.

"Callie, I'm glad to meet you," Mark said. "I met your Great Aunt Amelia when she was older than you are, but I can still see a family resemblance. You definitely have her auburn hair." He gestured for Callie and her mom to take a seat. "We had quite a search trying to locate you."

"What exactly led you to us, Mr. Hamilton?" Lee Anne said. "Amelia Calafont seems to have been my father-in-law's aunt, but as far as I know, he never met her. I found no mention of her in any family papers."

"That's really not too surprising," Bob interjected. "Your father-in-law was very young when his mother, Emily, died. She was Amelia's sister. He was raised by a stepmother and apparently lost track of his birth mother's family."

"That does not answer my mother's question," Callie said. "How were you able to track us?"

"Our search started with this picture we found in the Calafont home," Bob said, handing Callie the framed photograph of Emily and baby Matthew.

Callie smiled and turned to her mother. "Look, this must be Grandpa Matt when he was a baby. Isn't he cute?" she said.

When she turned the photo over, Callie thought the backing felt a little strange.

"I think there may be a piece of paper underneath this frame," she said, sliding the backing down.

Callie was right. There was a letter underneath the backing.

"Listen to this, Mom. It's really old. The date on it is 1947."

Callie read the letter aloud:

"Lawrence, Kansas

October 17, 1947

Dear Amelia,

What do you think of your nephew? Isn't he the prettiest baby that you have ever seen? Stephen gets impatient with me when I call Matt pretty. He says a boy should not be called 'pretty,' but I cannot help myself. I think he is pretty, don't you?

Do you think that Grandfather would be pleased with his namesake? I wish he would have lived to see him.

I must admit, I really love being a mother, but I am a little nervous at times. I am trying to follow the guidance of Dr. Spock but Stephen's mother keeps telling me to rely on my own judgment and instincts.

I like Kansas, but the open prairie is so different than the mountains of Pennsylvania. Stephen is taking his last classes for his engineering degree this semester at K.U. We are grateful that the G.I. Bill was there for him. He already has a job waiting for him at a firm in Kansas City.

How are you enjoying teaching? I am sure that you will be wonderful at it. You are good at any-thing that you do. I know that Mother and Father are glad to have you home, but I do worry that you may find it a little boring after the excitement of the war years in Washington, D.C. I hope you can move on from those years and put away any pain-ful memories. I know it will be hard for you to put the past behind you.

You need people your own age around you. I know you love our parents, but I don't want you to spend too much time in the old house with just Mom, Dad, and Tom for company.

All my love,

Emily"

Callie looked up from the paper and met Bob McPher-son's eyes opened wider with the mention of Tom.

"That's neat. I wonder who Tom is?" Callie said.

Bob still was not ready to buy into the ghost story, so he refrained from commenting. Instead, he turned to the older man to provide the answer.

Mark Hamilton, the man who just yesterday had lunch with the senate majority leader, cleared his throat.

"Tom, I believe, is the name of the ghost of the Confederate soldier the family believed lived in the old limestone house," he said.

"Are you telling me that we are inheriting a haunted house?" Lee Anne asked, a little incredulous and more than a little amused.

Lee Anne looked at Bob McPherson, who clearly was not buying into this ghost talk.

Mark Hamilton, however, surprised Lee Anne when he very seriously replied, "I believe you could say that is the case."

Callie had a one-word response: "Cool."

Fifteen

The Limestone House

June 11, 2011

The day after their visit to the attorneys' office, Lee Anne rented a car to drive to Pennsylvania for the official reading of the will. It was to be held in the library of the Calafont house.

Pulling up to the large historic home, Callie and Lee Anne were a little in awe. Their ten-year-old house in Kansas seemed not only new, but tiny, in comparison with the old limestone house.

Mark Hamilton's BMW was already in the driveway. He opened the door when they knocked. An older woman with salt and pepper hair was standing nervously behind him. Mark introduced them to Mamie Hodges and explained that she was also a beneficiary of the estate. He led them to the library, a wood-paneled room with wall-to-wall bookcases, straight out of a movie set. He suggested that they make themselves comfortable in the padded leather chairs as he took his place behind the large old walnut desk in the room. Mark Hamilton was an expert at putting people at ease. He knew just the right moment to end the small talk and remove the legal document from his briefcase.

"The Last Will and Testament of Amelia Stuart Calafont," he began. "I, Amelia Stuart Calafont, of Dickinson Township, of the County of Cumberland, and the Commonwealth of Pennsylvania, being of sound and disposing mind and memory, do hereby make, publish, and declare this to be my Last Will and Testament, hereby revoking all wills and codicils previously made by me."

The first clauses were standard, and Lee Anne was reminded of the reading of the wills after the plane crash. She pushed those thoughts out of her mind and returned to the present time and place as she listened.

"I leave and bequeath two hundred thousand dollars to Mrs. Mamie Hodges, in appreciation of her loyal service to me over the years. I also leave her my silver tea service. She spent many hours polishing it. In the unlikely event that she does not survive me, these bequests return to the estate."

At that point, Mamie Hodges proclaimed with tears in her eyes, "Miss Amelia was always so generous. She was just a great lady. I always loved that tea service."

Lee Anne thought, *I am glad that Mamie received this bequest. She seems like a nice woman.*

Mark continued, "I leave all of the tangible personal property that I may own at the time of my death, which is not otherwise specifically bequeathed under this will, including all land and residential property held under the Calafont name and the contents therein, to Mathew Calafont Monroe, the son of my beloved sister, Emily Calafont Monroe. If said Mathew Calafont Monroe does not survive me, this bequest should pass to his rightful descendants. In addition, I leave all my personal effects, household furniture and furnishings, books, silver, art objects, wearing apparel, jewelry, and other personal articles, not otherwise bequeathed, to said Matthew Calafont Monroe or his descendants.

At this point, as Lee Anne looked around the room, *Antiques Roadshow* came to mind. *The house is full of interesting pieces*, she thought. *With the adjoining land, we may actually inherit something of value.* She began to add up the amount of money owed in her outstanding bills and on her credit cards. *At the very least, we should be able to create a college fund for Callie and still have a little money left over to go toward our bills.*

"All stocks and bonds registered in the name of Amelia Calafont are included as part of this estate," Mark continued.

It took a moment for Lee Anne to absorb Mark's words. She looked at him and said, "Did Amelia have a large stock portfolio?"

"Well, you know the value of stocks and bonds fluctuate with the market, but conservatively, we estimate the value of Amelia's portfolio to currently be around six million dollars, give or take a few hundred thousand," Mark replied.

Neither Lee Anne nor Callie said anything. Their mouths just dropped open. They were in shock. Neither of them heard the remaining standard clauses that Mark was obliged to recite in order to bring the reading of the will to its official conclusion.

Tom had been listening to the reading of the will from a perch on the top of one of the bookcases. He looked down on the people seated in the library. He had watched them enter the room, and he recognized the lawyer as one of the men who visited the house a few months ago. However, it was the young girl who drew his attention. He moved closer to get a better look at her. She had to be Emily's great-granddaughter; there was no doubt at all. She was the spitting image of Miss Amelia when she was her age.

Tom could barely contain his excitement. When his spirit backed away from Callie, he accidently bumped into the library table with the large opened dictionary on top. The table and the dictionary fell to the floor.

Lee Anne and Callie jumped, but Mark and Mrs. Hodges were undisturbed. They had both wondered when Tom would make his presence known.

Sixteen

Just because Mark Hamilton read a will in an old lime-stone house in the Cumberland Valley did not mean that Lee Anne and Callie instantly became different people. They were too grounded in their Midwestern values. One hour did not erase a lifetime of living in a small university town in Kansas. However, there was no doubt about it; Amelia Calafont had just changed their lives.

Lee Anne and Callie were both quiet as they left the Calafont house to return to D.C. Lee Anne drove their rental car through the historic community of Carlisle before turning toward South Mountain. They passed through the small boroughs of Mt. Holly Springs and York Springs on their way to Route 15. On the other side of South Mountain, apple and peach orchards lined their route.

Along the way, and to her surprise, Callie saw Spanish signs on some of the buildings. It took her a moment to realize that these signs were intended for the migrant workers who picked the fruit crop. The land outside the car windows looked very different than the Kansas plains that stretched forever. Here, small mountains separated the land from the blue sky.

At almost the same moment, Lee Anne and Callie broke their silence. Callie got out her words first.

"What now, Mom? What do we do? We have enough money that we can do anything we want to do, but I have no idea what that means?" Callie said.

"I know," Lee Anne said. "I am just moving beyond the numb stage. I do know one thing; I'm hungry. Let's find some place to eat and talk."

For the two years since the plane crash, the mother and daughter had jointly made financial and other decisions. Usually, these decisions revolved around how to stretch their money until the next insurance check arrived. Lee Anne relied on her daughter's judgment. She knew that Callie had inherited her husband's intelligence and clearheadedness, and dealing with the tragedy of the plane crash gave her daughter a realistic picture of life, perhaps sometimes a little too realistic for a girl who was barely fifteen.

Lee Anne saw a small restaurant on their right as they reached Thurmont, Maryland. She pulled into the parking lot.

"Well, I know the first decision I'm going to make as an heiress," Callie proclaimed. "I'm going to order the largest hot fudge sundae on the menu!"

Lee Anne ordered a cup of coffee and a slice of pie, and then said, "I think we need to keep Amelia in our thoughts as we make plans. She obviously wanted her home to remain in the family. She could have sold her land at any time during the last thirty years to developers, but obviously she did not."

"I agree. I must admit, I did feel a connection to her home," Callie said. "Do you think we carry ancestral memories of a place in our DNA? Although, I don't think I want to live there all the time."

Lee Anne also felt no desire to relocate to Amelia's home.

"I'd like to visit it on weekends, perhaps like a vacation place, but I agree about living there year around," Lee Anne said. "I'm not averse to leaving Kansas, though. How do you feel about relocating to someplace where we could visit the house occasionally on weekends?"

"With Dad and Grandpa Matt gone, I have no strong ties to Lawrence," Callie said. "I'll be going to a new school this year anyway. It certainly does not have to be in Kansas."

Lee Anne thought for a moment. "I like the idea of living in a larger city. My main issue is your education. I want you to find a school that will nurture all your special gifts. What about a private school known for its academic programs? That is the one thing I really want for you, the chance to develop your great mind. I've not been able to give you all the opportunities that you deserve."

Callie got a little excited and said, "What about the D.C. area? I really like what we have seen of it. It still feels tied to Amelia. Remember the line in Emily's letter about Amelia living there during the War? We can move east and see if we like it. It will be an adventure! There must be some great schools around D.C."

"It would also put us close to Amelia's law firm and brokers," Lee Anne said. "I think we need their advice and guidance."

So, it was decided over ice cream and pie. Lee Anne and Callie Monroe were going to move across the country to the area that Great Aunt Amelia had called home. They were not particularly scared. They both felt free for the first time in years. At that moment, anything felt possible.

"Mom, do you think Aunt Amelia is my 'fairy godmother'?" Callie asked.

"I like that idea," Lee Anne said. "Although, your story is different than Cinderella's story. You do not need a prince charming to change your life. You can do that all on your own."

Seventeen

Ada Lovelace Academy

Fall 2011

So much needed to be done before the big move. There was no time to be lost if Callie was to be settled in a new school by the fall. While Lee Anne tended to the details of the move, Callie pored over catalogs of schools in the Washington, D.C., area. She kept returning to one catalog over and over again. It described a small private boarding school in the Virginia suburbs that catered to gifted young women.

Ada Lovelace Academy was no finishing school. Instead, it was a prestigious institution established to educate girls who showed great promise. The academy took its name from the beautiful nineteenth century English countess and mathematician who is considered the world's first computer programmer. The school did not just emphasize STEM disciplines. While the academy's catalog boasted of excellent science, technology, engineering, and math courses—some ADA girls went on to become doctors and engineers—the academy's founders valued creativity and imagination. So, Ada Lovelace Academy offered a wide range of courses designed to unlock the full potential of both the left and right brains of their girls.

The school's large endowment provided excellent facilities. Its computer and chemistry labs rivaled those found in major universities. Young musicians had the best acoustical practice rooms and played in the school's outstanding orchestra. Some girls brought the skills that allowed them to translate musical notes to finger positions on an instrument into their math and computer classes. Art classes brought out abilities needed to design websites and computer graphics. Ada Lovelace girls graduated with an appreciation for learning that went across the disciplines, and their degrees opened the doors to the best colleges and universities.

The girls were encouraged to play team sports. The official message on the field was that an Ada girl always tried her best and that trying mattered more than winning. However, many Ada girls were naturally competitive, and the school was known for its sports. Over the years, the Ada Lovelace soccer and lacrosse teams were considered the ones to beat among the local private schools. Even the dorms were designed with the school's values in mind. Four individual rooms, called a quad, shared a study space.

Callie loved the catalog description. It sounded perfect; however, the Ada Lovelace Academy did not accept everyone. Admittance was very competitive.

Lee Anne placed a call to Mark Hamilton for the lawyer's advice. It just happened that Kendall Blakely, the *Blakely* of Hamilton, Hamilton, and Blakely, served on the board of the Ada Lovelace Academy. He arranged for Callie to have an interview.

Callie and Lee Anne flew to the East Coast the first week of August to visit the school and meet with the admissions office.

When Callie actually saw the school buildings, she knew this was the school for her. She was on pins and needles as she awaited the results of her interviews. It did not take long for the school to make the decision. It was not just the Blakely connection that swayed the admissions office; Callie's innate intelligence, inquisitive mind, and levelheadedness made an impression on the interviewers. They knew that Callie Anne Monroe was meant to be an Ada Girl.

Jackie Hamilton took Lee Anne and Callie under her wing, now that Callie's future was settled and she and her mom were moving to Washington, D.C. The first thing she did was help them find a new three-bedroom condo in a renovated building in an up and coming area of Dupont Circle. Jackie had to reassure Lee Anne that despite the sticker shock she was experiencing when signing the closing papers, it was a reasonable price to pay for the house.

It took three months for Lee Anne to wrap up their life in Kansas and move into the condo. She was able to sell their house in Lawrence to a man who had just received a research grant at the university. Lee Anne shed a few tears as she packed up a lifetime of memories. There were a few more tears as she said goodbye to her coworkers at the library. She had lived in Kansas all of her life, and she would always cherish the memories of her time there.

Callie said goodbye to Brenna and her other friends, promising to keep in touch. She was excited about the possibilities that stretched before her, suddenly feeling very grown-up and looking forward to living in a dorm. She had been her mother's companion and helper since the plane crash, and although she knew that they would always share a close bond, it was a great relief to her that she no longer had to worry about her mother.

It had been three years since the plane crash. Lee Anne and Callie were ready to embrace their new life.

Eighteen

Ada Lovelace Academy was the perfect fit for Callie. She felt like a normal teenager, if you could consider someone with her intelligence normal. It did not matter that she was no longer the *best* student in her class. She now had to work at her studies, but she found that her mind expanded with the challenging classes.

The four quad–mates became best friends. They were an unlikely group. Callie was the shortest of the lot, but her thick auburn hair always made her stand out; her friends said that it was her best feature. Callie was grateful for her skin—her mother called it translucent—because unlike some kids, she had only endured two pimples in her life. In some ways, she was the most mature of the four girls because of her father's death. It made her grow up a little quicker than most.

Callie felt the closest to Madison. She was at least five inches taller than Callie and was the star forward on Ada's basketball team. She had the look of her Viking ancestors, with her long blonde hair. She made the others laugh by mimicking her great grandmother's Norwegian accent, which she had never actually heard. She usually sounded like her parents, who were originally from Cleveland. She was spontaneous and fun. Her nickname was 'Mad', which was not only a shortened version of her first name, but was given because of her frequent 'madcap' adventures.

Aimee and Megan rounded out the foursome. Aimee's skin was the color of a rich cup of black coffee laced with a little cream. She wore her curly brown hair in a short cut that showed off her big brown eyes. Her father, some sort of international financial expert, was currently stationed at the World Bank. Her accent was hard to place, as she had lived all over the world. She was gifted with a special ability to make a computer do what she wanted it to do. Megan still struggled with her 'baby fat', but despite the few extra pounds, she was a beauty, with raven hair that curled down her back. She did everything well, but she wasn't driven to make 'A's'; instead, she was always the lead in the school's musicals. She loved to sing and act, but her goal was to actually direct plays, not just star in them.

While academics were important, the girls always found time for fun. They became especially close with a group of boys that were friends of Madison's older brother, who attended school in the area. The tightknit group enjoyed going to the movies, playing tennis, and listening to music.

Callie spent her weeknights in her dorm room, but on weekends, she usually stayed in the Dupont Circle condo. It was good for her and her mother to separate.

The powerful connection they shared would always be there, but as the saying goes, *time heals all wounds.*

Both Lee Anne and Callie had moved beyond the incredible sadness they had felt with the unexpected loss of Callie's father. Lee Anne did not need Callie's support as much anymore, and she began to rely on her own judgment and the advice of new friends. It was healthy for all concerned that Lee Anne once again took on the role of the mother and Callie again became the daughter. Lee Anne also enjoyed hearing a sound that had been lost for far too long—the sound of Callie's laughter.

Lee Anne and Callie did not forget that they had Amelia Calafont to thank for their new life. As soon as the will was probated, Lee Anne arranged to have repairs made to the outside of the Calafont house. She convinced Mamie Hodges to become the Calafont house resident caretaker. Mamie loved the old house and cared for the rooms as if they were her own. The Calafont land also had to be maintained. Lee Anne hired Findley Quinn, a Cumberland County native, to take care of the land and the buildings. There was always something to keep him busy. Mr. Quinn and Mrs. Hodges got along well, as long as each one respected the other's domain.

Every three to four weeks, Lee Anne and Callie traveled to the Calafont house in Pennsylvania, where they were always welcomed by Mrs. Hodges with open arms. Lee Anne always stayed in the bedroom with the windows that faced the front yard, and Callie stayed in the room with the delicate chest of drawers.

Callie wondered about the chest in her room. It looked like it had always been there. She knew that it had once been Amelia's room, but Callie thought that the chest pre-dated Amelia. Mrs. Hodges told her that before it was Amelia's room, traditionally, it was the bedroom for the woman of the house.

Callie roamed the old house and absorbed the intricate details of its architecture. She loved the parlor with the baby grand piano. She had stopped her piano lessons when her father died, but she promised herself that she would start practicing again soon. Musical instruments are meant to be played, after all. Something about the parlor gave Callie a peculiar feeling, though. She almost felt as if she was being watched, and she wondered if air somehow had found a way to get into the old house. There were times when the curtains flared out and she felt a chill when she stood close to the old fireplace. It was strange.

In spite of these feelings, Callie was drawn to the old limestone house and looked forward to her weekends there.

Nineteen

Washington, D.C.

Spring 2013

Since getting the news of the inheritance, Lee Anne's countenance completely changed. No longer did her eyes show sadness and anxiety. Money may not buy happiness, but it did free Lee Anne from her constant anxiety about paying her bills. This freedom also allowed her to explore one of her dreams: to write children's books. As a children's librarian, she had seen the expression on the faces of the young children when they first read a special book. She could think of nothing better than creating books that caused such expressions.

Lee Anne established a home office in one of the bedrooms and quickly got to pursuing her dream. She was very disciplined with her writing, spending several hours a day honing her newfound passion. Although she enjoyed creating characters, she found it to be hard work, but she felt a degree of pride when she saw the words of her first book filling her computer screen.

By the spring of 2013, two years after the letter arrived in Kansas from Hamilton, Hamilton, and Blakely, Lee Anne and Callie were established in their new lives. Lee Anne was working with Bob McPherson to establish a trust for Callie, and the papers were ready for her to sign. Callie would take control of the funds when she turned twenty-one. By then, Lee Anne anticipated that her daughter would have completed her undergraduate degree and be ready for the next stage in her life, whatever that would be. Callie should have enough money to do anything that she wished. Lee Anne knew that she would use it wisely. Her daughter's Kansas upbringing still showed.

Lee Anne dressed carefully for her appointment at the law firm, examining herself in the full-length mirror. The previous week, she had gone shopping with Jackie Hamilton. Her new blue suit brought out the color of her eyes, and her stylish haircut was very flattering. Admiring her new look, she thought, *Well, I no longer look like a children's librarian. I can hold my own now with those women at Hamilton, Hamilton, and Blakely.* As she finished getting ready, she dabbed some perfume behind her ears and headed out into her new world. She didn't realize that the change in her appearance wasn't because of the new clothes she was wearing, but was because of the brightness in her blue eyes.

Bob McPherson immediately took notice of the changes in Lee Anne Monroe when she arrived at his new office, now located in the group of offices known in firm slang as *Partner's Row*. Six months earlier, he had officially made partner. He had worked hard to earn this position, and with it came perks and financial benefits. He liked the fact that his work had changed Lee Anne's and Callie's lives, so he kept them as his personal clients. As he shook Lee Anne's hand, he had a chance to assess her appearance. It was something he did regularly when he met a client, but this time it was different.

How did I miss how attractive Lee Anne Monroe is? he thought. However, his manner was extremely professional when he greeted her.

"It's good to see you again," Bob said. "I assume you've settled into your new life on the East Coast by now? I hope Callie's doing well. Has she adjusted to her new school?"

Lee Anne shared Callie's progress with him and commented briefly about their move from Kansas.

When the small talk was over, Bob turned to the business at hand. He went over the trust documents clause-by-clause and answered Lee Anne's appropriate and well thought out questions. Bob had her sign her name in the appropriate places and then gave her two copies, one for herself and one for Callie.

Bob didn't really want to see Lee Anne walk out the door just yet. He looked at the clock. At 4:30, it was early for him to wrap up his day. He knew that Washington's young professional crowd was already gathering at the local watering holes for happy hour. He surprised both of them with his next words.

"Can I buy you a glass of wine to celebrate?"

Lee Anne hesitated for just a second. She had not missed the look on Bob's face when she entered his office. It felt good to be appreciated as a woman by a successful, good-looking man. *One glass of wine won't hurt anything*, she thought.

The conversation flowed easily between Bob and Lee Anne. They caught up with the changes in their lives since they last talked. They covered Bob's promotion and Lee Anne's writing. After two glasses of wine, Bob suggested dinner. He knew a nice place around the corner. Over dinner, she shared with Bob how much she liked her new condo. She told him that Jackie Hamilton had helped her decorate it.

"We've become really good friends," Lee Anne said. "Jackie has made my transition to this new world so much easier. When I first met her, I was a little intimidated. She seemed so cosmopolitan, but now that I know her better, I find her one of the most genuine people that I've ever met."

Bob refrained from saying out loud what he was thinking—*So, why didn't Jackie arrange for us to sit together at one of her famous dinner parties then?* —and instead just laughed.

"You and I share an appreciation for Mark's wife," Bob said. "You can't tell me anything I don't already know about how kind Jackie can be. She even got me up on one of her horses. She looks for people to convert to horseback riding because Mark hates horses. He fell off one when he was a boy and refused to follow the old adage of getting right back on it. I love getting out of the city and spending time at the Hamilton's. Unfortunately, my work gets in the way and I just can't do it as often I wish."

Lee Anne understood what he meant. "I love living in the city also. There is so much to see and do in Washington, but sometimes I need a break from its intensity. Callie and I are very lucky. We have the Calafont house when we need to escape."

"I have thought about that old house often. I was only there once, but my visit to it stayed with me," Bob said.

"You must visit it again. Why don't you join us in Pennsylvania some weekend?" Lee Anne said.

Clearly, Lee Anne was not just being polite, but was serious about the invitation.

"I'll take you up on that offer," Bob said. "I would love to see the house again."

"So, let's try for a Saturday in the Cumberland Valley this summer," Lee Anne said.

She looked at the time and was surprised to see that it was almost ten p.m.

Bob flagged down a cab to take her home and then went back to his office. There were still a few documents demanding his attention before the next morning. The late evening was a small price to pay for such an enjoyable dinner.

Twenty

Ada Lovelace Academy

Memorial Day Weekend, 2013

Callie was finishing up her a math assignment on the Friday afternoon before the Memorial Day weekend. When she took a break, it hit her that two years ago, she was bored with her life, but then a letter arrived from Hamilton, Hamilton, and Blakely, and everything changed because of a woman she never met named Amelia Calafont. Not for the first time did Callie think, *I wish I knew more about my fairy Godmother.* She obviously had been a woman ahead of her times. What did Emily mean in her letter when she wrote Amelia about *"the excitement of the war years in Washington, D.C.?"*

Her thoughts also turned to Tom, the spirit who many people said haunted the Calafont house. Was it possible that the house was truly haunted? Callie wasn't able to explain away the unusual feelings and occurrences that she experienced there. And she knew that Mamie Hodges, as traditional as they came, accepted Tom's presence as a reality. Callie asked her about the idea of a ghost and, Mrs. Hodges had told her, without any doubt in her voice, that Tom's spirit had lived in the house since 1863.

Could a Confederate soldier really haunt her ancestral home? Callie's logical mind had a difficult time wrapping her head around the idea, but she knew that tables did not just fall over by themselves.

Just as an idea took hold in Callie's brain, Madison popped into her room. Her friend was always ready to try a new experiment.

"Mad, how would you like to spend June ghost hunting?" Callie said.

Madison's mouth dropped open, but her reply was in character: "Wow, sounds like fun!"

Callie checked with her mother to get her approval for her and Mad to spend June in Pennsylvania. Her mom agreed to the idea without reservation, perhaps because Callie did not bother to mention their plans for ghost hunting.

When Lee Anne called Mrs. Hodges to tell her that the two girls were coming, the older woman immediately began planning for their stay, cleaning two of the bedrooms thoroughly, even though the rooms were already clean. Mamie Hodges did not tolerate dust in any of her rooms!

Tom overheard the housekeeper's end of the phone conversation with Lee Anne. He could barely wait for Callie and Madison to arrive. It would be just like having

Amelia and Emily in the house again. *If it is my destiny to be trapped in this house,* he thought, *then I want some interesting young people around me.*

Part III

Twenty-one

The Limestone House

June 2013

Madison was the proud owner of a used Honda Civic, given to her by her father on her sixteenth birthday. Callie's mother and her father gave them stern lectures about not talking to strangers and driving carefully.

"If I hear that you and Madison are letting Mrs. Hodges wait on you hand and foot, I'll come up and take both of you back to D.C. with me," Lee Anne said sternly in her Midwestern tone. "I don't care how much money you inherited from Aunt Amelia; you know your way around a house and a kitchen. I expect you to remember it this summer."

Still, the girls felt very independent when they left the D.C. area to drive to Pennsylvania. Callie planned for them to leave at two in the afternoon, but she should have known better. Madison always ran late. So, it was after four in the afternoon before Mad crossed the Maryland line on their way to Cumberland County. For sentimental reasons, Callie had Madison stop at the restaurant in Thurmont where, two years ago, she and her mother made plans.

The girls had not eaten since lunch, so Mad ordered a sandwich and Callie a cheeseburger. After they ate their meal, the girls shared a hot fudge sundae in honor of Aunt Amelia. It was just as good as Callie remembered.

As the girls were relaxing and talking on their drive, Callie suddenly realized that it was getting late. They'd need to hurry if they were going to get to the Calafont house before dark. Turning north toward South Mountain, Callie shared with Madison the story of her surprise inheritance.

"It sounds like a Disney movie," Madison said. "So, Amelia haunts her former home? She is the one we are supposed to find?"

"No, as far as we know, Amelia is comfortably situated in her next life. Although I do want to find out more about her. There is a bit of a mystery associated with her story. We don't really know what she did during WWII or how she became a multimillionaire. She's not our ghost, however."

"So, who's the ghost?" Madison asked.

"A Confederate soldier named Tom," Callie said.

"You must be kidding," Madison said, almost driving off the road.

"Be careful. I don't want to have to call my mom to tell her that we had an accident before we even made it to the Pennsylvania line," Callie cautioned Madison.

Mamie Hodges greeted Callie and Madison warmly with a hug when the girls arrived around seven p.m. As soon as she helped them carry their suitcases inside the house, she insisted that they eat the chicken salad she'd made, and she had homemade brownies for dessert, fresh out of the oven.

Callie smelled the chocolate the minute she entered the kitchen. It was her one true weakness. Although it really had not been that long since the hot fudge sundae, the salad tasted great. She also allowed herself one brownie.

After the girls finished eating, Mrs. Hodges led them up to two rooms on the second floor. Callie again stayed in the room that Amelia had once called her own, and Madison put her suitcase down in what had once been Emily's room. After the long drive to Pennsylvania from the D.C. area, the girls were exhausted. Callie barely had the energy to call her mother to tell her of their safe arrival. Both girls collapsed on their designated beds and Callie was asleep as soon as she closed her eyes.

The next morning, Callie awoke early to the sounds of birds in the trees. She sat up and looked around the room. It still felt like Amelia's room. There were little signs of her great aunt all over the place, including her comb and brush set on the dresser. Callie thought of the old woman with white hair and bright inquisitive eyes that she had seen in pictures. Again, she thought, *Thank you, Amelia, for everything. I want to get to know you this summer.*

When Callie heard Madison in the next room, she went over and knocked on her door.

"Wow," Madison said, "I slept like a baby! Is this a homemade quilt on the bed? It sure is comfortable."

"It probably is," Callie said. "Hey, let's get something to eat and then explore. I'm starving. Is that bacon I smell?"

Mamie Hodges was at the stove turning over blueberry pancakes when the girls entered the kitchen. She glowed when they paid her compliments. She loved that she had people to care for once again, not just empty rooms.

As much as Callie enjoyed being waited on, she remembered her mother's warning. She knew her mother was capable of carrying out her threat if she thought she was taking advantage of Mrs. Hodges.

After three pancakes, bacon, orange juice, and a glass of milk, Callie was full, so when Mrs. Hodges tried to push another pancake her way, she said, "I cannot put one more bite in my mouth, Mrs. Hodges. It was *so* good, but if I eat like this all summer, I will go back to school two sizes larger! My mother said that if you cook for us, we have to do the dishes and clean the kitchen. Just sit down now and talk to us while we make short work of these tasks."

Mamie enjoyed listening to the girls talk. The house-keeper was truly looking forward to the summer, knowing how fun it was going to be having young people in the old house.

Twenty-two

Callie and Madison decided that the best way to start the day was to unpack and then explore the house's nooks and crannies. In the formal dining room, there was a large walnut table surrounded by six heavy chairs. Callie noticed the chair covers right away. An earlier Calafont woman had spent many hours on their beautiful needlepoint design.

"I certainly did not inherit that ability. I'd never have the patience for that intricate needlework," Callie said.

The china cabinet housed three different sets of china. Callie imagined that each one represented the personal style of an earlier Calafont woman. She knew that tradition called for women to select a china pattern when they got married. Callie thought it was a nice idea, but she was not sure that it fit with today's lifestyle.

The china also caught Mad's eyes. "Those dishes are very pretty, but I'd be scared to try to drink from those teacups. I'd probably drop one and break it into a thousand pieces. Give me stoneware any day, especially since it can go in a dishwasher," Mad said.

"I know," Callie said. "This house takes me back to a previous century. Not the twentieth, the nineteenth. I love the china, the quilts, and the delicate antiques, but sometimes I think modern living is a whole lot easier."

It was a beautiful June day, and the girls headed outside to explore. Callie knew that June could be hot in Central Pennsylvania, but this day was almost perfect, in the low eighties.

Thanks to Mr. Quinn, the Calafont yard was glorious. It had rained the previous week and the yard had the healthy green look of well-tended grass that had plenty of water. Next to the house, a few late red azaleas were blooming, and outside the parlor windows, a large white snowball bush was flourishing. Callie showed Madison the rose garden on the other side of the house, close to the sunroom. Some of the roses were just beginning to bloom, and Callie could not resist bending down to smell the fragrant buds.

The girls walked toward the ancient barn, about a half a mile from the house. Purple irises lined the path. The barn looked like it had been there for hundreds of years. Callie's ancestors had built its foundation from old stones that matched the house. Callie had never seen this type of barn in Kansas, but they were all over Pennsylvania. She now knew they were called German bank barns. She admired their practical design. The two-level barn was built into the side of a hill, thus allowing both the first and second floor to be ground level.

Mr. Quinn was outside the barn sharpening some tools.

"The yard looks beautiful," Callie said. She then introduced him to Madison.

"It's nice to meet you. I sure hope you girls have a good summer. We just had an addition to the barn yesterday. You might want to check it out. Just go inside and have a look."

Both girls were curious and had no idea what they would see inside the barn. On the other side of the door, a large goat was chewing on some hay. Beside her, there was a small new brown and white kid, standing on four wobbly feet.

"Oh, have you ever seen anything cuter, Madison?" said Callie. "Would it be all right if we pet it?" Callie asked.

"Just be gentle," Mr. Quinn said. He watched closely as the two girls cooed and awed over the new baby.

Callie looked again at Mr. Quinn. He seemed so much a part of this place, as if he just sprouted from the land like a weed that grew up in the middle of a corn field. She could not picture how Quinn's wizened face had looked in his younger days.

"Did you grow up around here, Mr. Quinn?" Callie asked.

"Born and Bred in the valley," he responded.

"Then you must have known Aunt Amelia," Callie said.

"She was my third-grade school teacher. Best teacher I ever had," he said. "She made science real for us. We did experiments even in grade school. She not only made us learn our multiplication tables, but she also taught us what they meant and how to use them in our daily world. She was something else. She knew everything."

Including how to make the best stock market picks, Callie thought to herself.

Twenty-three

That evening Callie and Madison convinced Mrs. Hodges to continue the practice they had started at breakfast. She did the cooking and the girls washed and dried the dishes and cleaned the kitchen. Afterwards, the two girls relaxed in the room with the large piano. Callie was always drawn to this old-fashioned room. Her eyes fixed on the large oil painting of the two girls above the mantle. Callie knew that the younger one was Emily, Grandpa Matt's mother. Her hair was a rich dark brown color, but Callie could not take her eyes off the older girl. It was Amelia. Callie's eyes focused on her hair—the same as her own dark red hair.

"Wow, that girl looks just like you," Madison said, amazed, coming up from behind.

All her life, Callie had felt different from everyone else in her family. Her red hair seemed to come from nowhere, just a loose piece of DNA that somehow found its way into her "hair gene." Now, looking at Amelia's portrait, she felt connected to her father's family in a powerful way.

Madison's words interrupted her reverie.

Not really buying into the idea that there was an unsettled spirit upon them, Madison whispered loudly, clearly being a little facetious, "When do I get to see the ghost?"

Callie felt she was obliged to defend the family story, although she had her own doubts about the reality of Tom's spirit living among them.

"It's not that we can just conjure him up on a whim," Callie said. "Just wait, furniture has a way of moving by itself in this house."

Listening in, Tom thought to himself, *I'll let the girls settle down and then I'll surprise them.*

Callie moved over to the piano that dominated much of the room. She touched the keys and played a few notes. It had a wonderful tone. Family pictures were displayed on the old instrument. She knew that Bob McPherson originally found the photograph of Emily and Grandpa Matt among these pictures. She left the keyboard and studied the arrangement of photos on the piano. She picked up the picture of a bridal couple. She recognized the bride as Emily, the young mother in the photo with baby Matt. The groom was a good-looking military officer with wings on his uniform. Callie knew this meant that he had been a pilot in World War II. So, this man, her great-great grandfather, started the tradition of Monroe men flying above the clouds. He died before she was born. It was as if she was holding her own story in her hands. She felt emotional and more than a little foolish as she pushed back the tears that came to her eyes.

Once again, Madison came up behind Callie and interrupted the moment, lessening its intensity for Callie.

"I know that I am supposed to be a science geek, but I find old pictures and the history behind them really interesting. There are some wonderful photos here. I can enjoy them even though they are not my family," Madison said.

Callie looked at her with new appreciation. Some Ada girls might not have appreciated the photos. Callie was very glad that she had selected Madison as the friend to share her adventure this summer—and there was no doubt in her mind that it was going to be *quite* the adventure!

Madison picked up a photo that was tucked behind the Calafont wedding and baby pictures. It was much older than the World War II era photos.

"Hey, I bet this is a daguerreotype. I read about them in one of my science classes about light and photography. It was an early photographic process that actually printed an image on silver-plated copper," Madison said, in awe that she was actually holding one.

Callie looked at the image Madison was holding. A pretty blonde woman in a long skirt was sitting on a chair. A man in a soldier's uniform stood behind her. Callie thought it was a picture from the Civil War era. She studied it for a moment.

"Why is it that men in uniform seem to like having their picture taken?" Callie said. "I wonder if it's because they worry that they might not make it, and with a photo, they'll live forever?"

Looking at the picture more closely, Callie felt goose bumps appear on her arm.

"Madison, look at this. I know this is a black and white image, but do you think it is possible that this man's uniform is gray?"

Madison again took the picture from Callie and stared at it.

"Yes, I think he may be wearing a Confederate uniform," Madison said. She tuned the picture over and read aloud, "Mattie and Tom, first anniversary, May 22, 1861."

Callie grabbed her friend's arm, "Madison, don't you know what this means?" She said excitedly. "Tom, the Confederate soldier, really existed!"

"Wait a second, Callie," Madison said. "Just because he existed once does not mean that his spirit now haunts this house."

Tom listened carefully. *These modern girls will sure be hard to convince. I guess I will have to enter into this discussion in a dramatic way.*

He contemplated the best way to do it. It had been fifty or so years since Tom had last materialized. With only Amelia in the house, he had no need to exert himself in that way. Tom's spirit and Amelia knew how to communicate with each other without Tom taking a material form. He was rusty. Madison and Callie obviously needed to open their sophisticated minds to new possibilities. He would have to practice and show himself at just the right time. For now, it should be sufficient for him to make his presence known in a small way. He bumped into the big comfortable chair that stood beside the piano and moved it five inches closer to the musical instrument, causing Madison to take a step back and trip over it.

"I didn't realize that I was standing so close to that chair," Madison said.

"Didn't I tell you about the furniture? See, what I mean." Callie said and left it at that.

Madison just looked at her and said, "On that note, I think I am going to head off to bed."

Callie joined her. As they walked up the stairs, Callie hummed aloud the notes from the theme song to the *Twilight Zone*.

Twenty-four

The Limestone House

Summer 1943

Tom's spirit moved closer to the piano when the girls left the room. He was very pleased that his wedding picture was among the Calafont family photos. He remembered the day that Amelia placed the daguerreotype there. It was the day after Matthew Calafont's funeral.

It was the summer of 1943. America was in the middle of another war. Amelia and Emily were briefly together again. In the fall, Emily was to begin her last year at Bryn Mawr. Amelia was no longer living at home. She did not really talk about her work in Washington, D.C., but her family was proud that she was doing her part for the war effort. There were no Calafont sons to lend to the cause, but Amelia's work was important; at least that is what she told her family without offering any details. She came home on leave as soon as she received her mother's call about their grandfather.

The family was deluged with outpourings of sympathy. Anna, Amelia's mother, was a frail woman. Regardless, she always fulfilled her duty to her family. Her father-in-law's passing touched many people in Central Pennsylvania. She spent the last three days saying the appropriate words to the many friends and neighbors who called on the old limestone house. It was draining. After the viewing, the funeral, the graveside service, and the mandatory reception at the Calafont house, Anna was exhausted. After the last visitor left the house, she escaped to her bedroom to lie down. Never comfortable with emotion, her husband, Robert, retreated to his office at Cumberland Mutual Trust. Amelia and Emily were left alone downstairs.

The two girls finally were able to relax after their taxing day. It was hard work being gracious to all who came out to honor their grandfather.

Emily broke the companionable silence first. "It was nice that Mr. Hamilton came up from Washington for the funeral. I know that he has been our family lawyer for years, but I think Grandfather was more than just a client to him. His son sure looked polished in his navy whites. When was Bill Hamilton promoted to lieutenant commander? His gold oak leaf looked new."

"His promotion must have been recent. The last time I saw him, he still had lieutenant bars," Amelia said.

Emily looked at her sister closely. "So, you have seen him recently? I thought I picked up on something. He seemed to be here to see you more than to honor Grandfather. His eyes did not leave you all afternoon. What's the story there?"

"Oh, Bill has been very attentive since I moved to Washington. He has taken me out to dinner, and it is hard to turn down a man in uniform who wants to feed you. But a few weeks ago, he asked me to marry him. It would be so easy to say yes. Our families have all these long-standing ties, and I know Grandfather would have liked it. Bill is probably headed out to the Pacific soon. I feel it is almost my duty as an American to marry him before he leaves. But there is something that holds me back. He's a very nice man, but there are just no sparks. There are supposed to be, aren't there?" Amelia paused for a moment. "I want more than nice, at least a little excitement. It cannot be enough that he takes me out to dinner and that he looks good in his uniform."

"Well, Amelia, I believe in sparks. I know they can exist," Emily said.

"What do you mean? Why Emily, you are almost glowing. Tell me about him," Amelia said.

"I have wanted to tell you about him for months, but I have been a little afraid that if I talk about him, I might jinx it. I met him at a USO dance right before he deployed. We only had four weeks before he was sent to England. He is in the Army Air Corps. He's flying missions over Europe. I don't know the details, but I imagine that he's bombing Germany. You know his letters are always read by military censors to make sure that he doesn't accidently leak secrets. We write almost every day. We're going to get married as soon as the war is over."

Amelia reached out to hug her baby sister. "I am so happy for you. You still have not told me his name."

"Stephen Monroe. Emily Monroe has a nice ring to it, don't you think? He's originally from Kansas. He was working on an engineering degree at the University of Kansas when the war started, but he plans to return and finish his education. He wants me to go with him. I don't even allow myself to think that he may not come home. Our dreams are just too real not to come true."

The girls were both quiet for a moment, lost in thought about the realities of the world-wide war.

"Let's put the war out of our minds for a bit and put some order in this room," Amelia said, breaking their silence. "You know Mother. She will be overwhelmed when she comes down if she sees this mess. Let's see what we can do to help her out."

Amelia thought for a moment. "I know. Let's make a list of the people who sent flowers. Mother will want to send thank-you notes as soon as possible."

Amelia began the process of taking the cards off the numerous bouquets of flowers.

"Emily, I'll read the names on the cards and you can write them down. Let's work in the library. We can sit at Grandfather's desk."

Amelia sat in her grandfather's chair and Emily sat in front of the large walnut desk. Amelia began reading the names and Emily carefully wrote them down. As they finished the task, Amelia's eyes were drawn to the two pictures on the desk. One was a black and white picture of her great-grandmother, Sarah. Color photography did not exist in the 1870s, when the picture was taken, and she wished that she could see the color of Sarah Calafont's hair. Her grandfather always told her that she had his mother's hair.

Her eyes were drawn to the picture that stood next to Sarah Calafont's photograph. She knew that it was taken some place far away from the Cumberland Valley, a decade earlier than Sarah's picture. The man in the Confederate uniform pictured in the daguerreotype was as much a part of her family lore as her great-grandmother's red hair.

"Look, Emily. It's the picture of Tom and Mattie. I felt his presence today. Did you?"

"Yes, Tom was definitely here. You know, I tried to tell one of my friends about Tom's spirit living in this house, but she looked at me as if I were crazy. Remember when Grandfather showed us this photo and he told us the story of the night that Tom died? It's such a sad story. I used to feel a little guilty that I was secretly glad that Tom could not move on to the afterlife. It was such fun to have him as a playmate when we were little," Emily confessed.

"I know. Remember those tea parties? I have always loved this picture of Tom and Mattie. Do you think it would be all right if I moved it to the piano so I can see it when I play? Tom always seemed to enjoy listening to me sing," Amelia said.

"I think it would be the right place for it," Emily said.

Tom's spirit watched Amelia and Emily rather ceremoniously carry the daguerreotype to the parlor and place it on the back of the piano. They looked at the family photographs arranged on the musical instrument. Tom and Mattie belonged there.

Twenty-five

The Limestone House

June 2013

As Callie was getting ready for bed, she took her nightgown out of the chest of drawers with the curved legs. She was learning to appreciate the antiques in the house and wondered about the history of this piece of furniture.

Before she settled under the covers, she opened the drawer of the night stand beside her bed to store her watch. She noticed a folded piece of paper on the bottom of the drawer. When she unfolded it, she saw a note written in cursive. The writing seemed to be that of an older person. It took a moment for Callie to get used to the sprawling writing style.

For the second time in one evening, she felt tears in her eyes. The note was obviously written by Amelia shortly before she died.

Today is my 93rd birthday. I am in the tenth decade of my time on this earth.

My life is slipping away. I feel that the end is approaching. I can no longer play music now that my hands are so wrinkled and crippled. Without music, life loses so much of its beauty. Music gave me so much joy these last years as I lived in this big house without human company. Now that this joy has left me, I know that my Lord is calling me home. I look forward to hearing the heavenly chorus.

I find myself thinking about the past now, seldom the present, and never the future. It is the war years that my mind returns to over and over again. It was exciting to be part of something bigger than myself. We girls all took our oath of secrecy so seriously that even now I cannot write details about that experience. I am proud of my work during those years and know that it made a difference. I think of Michael and how he made me laugh. His brown eyes always had a twinkle in them when he teased me. I am grateful for the five months we had together. Some people live their whole lives without knowing that type of love.

I know that there are people in this community that I taught who now have grandchildren. I hope some will remember the lessons of my classroom and pass them on to their descendants. Perhaps a few found that information can be fun and used their knowledge to solve life's puzzles, as I did.

Callie read Amelia's words over several times, until she could almost recite them. She stored them inside her, not only in her brain but in that part of a person's being where love and emotion live. The words became part of Callie, as if she had written them herself. Tonight, when she looked at Amelia's portrait, she felt very connected to her great aunt. Now, it was as if Amelia had left this letter for her to find. She felt her Aunt Amelia was speaking directly to her. Amelia's note generated additional questions in Callie's mind about the woman who changed her life. Callie wondered about Michael and Amelia's work during the war.

Apparently, Callie shared more than just red hair with her great aunt. Callie had an innate gift for mathematics that she clearly did not inherit from her mother, who had trouble balancing her checkbook. Amelia apparently also understood how numbers worked. Her stock portfolio indicated it. Like Callie, Amelia liked to solve puzzles. She must have gotten some of her abilities from Amelia. No one who knew Amelia indicated that there was anything wrong with her mental faculties, yet she believed in the existence of Tom's spirit. If Amelia believed in Tom's existence, it was good enough for Callie.

Callie thought of the last lines of Amelia's note. Perhaps she could repay her benefactor by learning Tom's story and, in doing so, helping Tom's spirit find rest. She owed it to Amelia to try her best to bring peace to this house. She also knew that she had something that Amelia did not have. She had the internet.

Twenty-six

Callie woke up later than usual the next morning. She had not slept well. Amelia's story played out in her dreams. She dressed quickly and set out to find Madison to tell her about the note. Her friend was in the kitchen talking with Mrs. Hodges. Obviously, Madison already had finished another one of the housekeeper's large meals. Callie turned down the offer of a big breakfast and just gulped down some orange juice and a couple of pieces of toast. She was impatient to talk with Madison, so she made a quick task of the breakfast cleanup and turned to her friend.

"Mad, let's go for a walk. I need to tell you something."

Madison was a little surprised at Callie's early morning intensity, but she went along with her friend. They walked through the trees toward the creek on the edge of Calafont land. By the time they reached the stream, her friend had repeated, almost verbatim, the contents of Amelia's note.

"Clearly, our ghost really existed for Amelia," Callie said. "We both know that there are unusual currents here. I feel that Amelia wants me to bring peace for Tom. I owe her that much. I just know that is what I am supposed to do. Don't ask me to explain it all. Will you help me?"

Callie was afraid that she sounded crazy, but hoped her friend would understand.

"Wow, I don't really get it all, but you are right, spooky things happen here. Let's see what we can find out," Madison said, up for the challenge.

"Oh, that's great! Listen, Madison, I have an idea. Remember Mr. Olson's principles of research class? He taught us the *scientific method for problem solving*. Who says that systematic approach is limited to mathematical theorems and chemistry experiments? I think we can use that methodology to find out about our ghost."

Madison brightened. Not only was Mr. Olson her favorite teacher, but she had gotten an A in his class. She could put her head around the idea of scientific experimentation. She paused, trying to remember the steps outlined in the teacher's lectures.

"Olson always talked about the importance of first articulating the problem," Madison said. "He said that if you cannot state the problem, then you are not ready to begin. I remember his observation that many projects do not result in changing things because they started with the wrong questions."

"That's right, Madison. You know, I am having a difficult time in separating my desire to find out more about Amelia with the details about our ghost. I think we could use a bulletin board like they do on the crime dramas on TV. We can divide it into two sides: Tom's Story and Amelia's Story. Underneath, we can put yellow sticky notes with the details that we know about each."

Callie was on a roll now, talking as she put her head around her ideas. She was eager to get started.

"We need supplies," Callie suggested. "Let's drive to Carlisle. There's a Staples in the shopping center."

On their way to Carlisle in Madison's car, they saw several large blue Pennsylvania historic signs about the Battle of Gettysburg. They read that Confederate regiments passed this way. The fact that this famous battle was part of the local history intrigued Callie. In Kansas, local Civil War history meant "Bleeding Kansas" and border warfare. The big battles happened elsewhere.

"It gives me chills to think that our house looked much the same during the Battle of Gettysburg as it does now," Callie said. "Just think, my Calafont ancestors were living here then. They must have been scared. The Confederates were invading their land."

An idea hit her with a bang. Tom may have been in one of those regiments.

"Madison, we need to study the troop movements of the Confederates in this part of the country. I remember reading that most Civil War regiments were made up of people from one particular state, and then within that regiment, companies were created by county. If we can find out where the troops came from that marched through Calafont land, we may be able to identify some potential leads regarding Tom's background."

"Well, I think Mr. Olson would have called that an 'hypothesis.' So, let's figure out how we go about proving or disproving this theory," Madison said.

"Before we go home, let's stop at a library and check out some history books on Gettysburg and the war. Mr. Olson always told us that we need to start by doing background research. Mom and I noticed a library in Mt. Holly Springs. It looks really neat from the outside, and I've been wanting to visit it," Callie said.

The outside of the Amelia Givin library reminded Callie of a castle. It was just as dramatic inside. The beautiful carved woodwork had almost a Middle Eastern design. When she and Madison asked about the history of the building, the woman behind the desk was eager to elaborate.

"The library is a gift from Amelia Givin to the people of Mt. Holly Springs. Her family made a fortune from the paper mill in town, and she thanked the workers by giving them this library. She was an exceptional person. In the 1890s, she ran her family's business as a single woman, three decades before women had the right to vote."

There must be something special about the name Amelia. Is it only given to unique women ahead of their time? Callie thought.

The librarian pointed Madison and Callie to the section dedicated to Civil War history, where they selected several books on the subject. Callie noticed that one writer, Mark Nesbitt, had even created a series titled *Ghosts of Gettysburg*. Callie completed the paperwork for a library card and selected several books to take with her.

Madison had to slow her car to a crawl on their way back to the Calafont house, as a horse-drawn buggy driven by an Amish man was in front of them.

"Between the Calafont house with its Confederate ghost, the beautiful library, and now the buggy, I am beginning to feel that we lost the twenty-first century," Callie said. "I need to get the current century back!"

"Yeah, I know what you mean," Madison said as she pulled into the Calafont driveway.

Soon, the girls were back in their own world, using their cell phones to text Aimee and Megan.

Twenty-seven

The morning after their library visit, Callie and Madison turned the sunroom into their "war room," as Madison called it. They placed the two bulletin boards they bought the previous day against one of the walls. They labeled one *Amelia* and the other *Tom*. Following Mr. Olson's guidelines, they developed an hypothesis for each person and divided each board into three areas: Know, Guess, Questions. They wrote on stickies and placed the stickies underneath the headers.

Madison had taken a calligraphy class the previous year and wrote the words in a neat script.

Callie placed photos of Amelia around her board. There was a baby picture of Amelia on the lap of a woman Callie assumed was her great-great grandmother. Callie had seen her own baby picture and thought that even as babies, she and Amelia looked alike. Next to the baby picture, she placed a picture of Amelia and Emily, both sitting on a horse, around 1930. These images were all black and white. Without the portrait above the mantel, Callie would not have realized that she and Amelia shared auburn hair. The available pictures of Amelia jumped to the late 1960s, when she was teaching school and her head was already covered by white hair. Callie was frustrated. She wanted to see the Amelia of her twenties, when she was working in D.C. and in love with Michael.

It was almost two in the afternoon when the girls stepped away from their boards and proudly admired their artistic handiwork. Last year, the girls had created an exhibit for their history day project. They knew how to put a board together.

"Well, it sure looks pretty," Callie said, "but art is not really our purpose. Remember the rule we always heard about National History Day entries: content, not beauty, is king. We have many more questions than facts, so now, we need to put our heads together to think about our next steps and how we get answers."

Callie picked up one of the books on the Battle of Gettysburg that she checked out of the library. She read about the Confederates under Ewell, who marched north. Callie sat up straight in her chair. It appeared that one of his divisions, led by a General Rodes, marched through this area of the Cumberland Valley.

"Hey, Madison, I think I found something!" Callie exclaimed. She read aloud from her book.

Madison pulled out her phone. She was an expert in searching the internet. "You're right, Callie. It looks like we should be paying attention to one of the brigades in Rodes' Division. If I had to place my bets, I would say that Ramseur's Brigade is a likely candidate. Although Iverson's is also a possibility. I cannot find a listing of the specific men in either group, so I'm not sure where we go from here."

AMELIA

HYPOTHESIS

Amelia worked on a top-secret government project, where she developed skills that helped her become an investor. She fell in love with Michael, who probably died during World War II. She came home heartbroken and spent her life teaching.

KNOW

Born: July 18, 1918
Died: Sept. 27, 2010
Born and died in the Calafont house, Cumberland County, PA
Worked in D.C. during WW II; returned to PA and taught school
Loved Michael
Invested in the stock market
Played the piano and loved music
One sister, Emily

GUESS

Her job in D.C. helped the war effort

QUESTIONS

What did she do during the war?
What happened to Michael?
How did she get to be an investor?

TOM

HYPOTHESIS

Tom died during the Confederate invasion of the North, during the Gettysburg Campaign, perhaps close to the Calafont house. Because no one knew who he was, and his loved ones were unable to say goodbye, his soul cannot find peace and he is restless. If we can find out more about his story and honor it, perhaps his soul can move to the afterlife.

KNOW

Born?
Died?
Fought for the Confederate States of America
    during the Civil War
Married Mattie on May 22, 1860

GUESS

Died in Pennsylvania during the Gettysburg
    Campaign
May have marched in front of the Calafont house

QUESTIONS

What is his last name?
What was his regiment?
Where is he from?

Right at that moment, the girls heard Mrs. Hodges in the kitchen.

The housekeeper knew that after all their hard work, the teenagers would be hungry. She pulled out her mixer and soon had a batch of chocolate chip cookie dough ready. She was putting the first batch in the oven when Callie and Madison bounded into the kitchen.

"Do you two want to lick the bowl?" Mrs. Hodges asked, handing each girl a beater.

The girls' tongues quickly found pieces of the dough left on the beaters. It was so much fun to act like little kids again.

Callie touched a stray chocolate chip still in the bowl and popped it into her mouth.

"The dough is almost as good as the baked cookie!" Madison exclaimed.

"It's great, but nothing beats the melted chocolate in an actual cookie," Callie declared.

The smell of the cookies permeated the room as Mrs. Hodges pulled the first hot baking sheet from the oven. The two girls barely waited for the cookies to cool before they each grabbed one.

"You girls need more than sugar," Mrs. Hodges said. "There's ham in the refrigerator for sandwiches."

"I'll make a sandwich for each of us," Callie said, jumping up from her seat. "You just sit down and relax."

Callie soon had the sandwiches ready to accompany the cookies.

"How is your work going?" Mrs. Hodges said.

"We're getting a good start, but we have a lot more questions than answers," Callie said after washing down another cookie with a sip of milk.

"By the way, do you know if there are more family pictures around? I would love to have some pictures of Amelia in her twenties, during World War II? Did she ever talk about those years with you?" Callie asked.

"Never," said Mrs. Hodges. "I did not start working for her until she was getting on in years. Miss Amelia was interested in everything. Why, even when I came to clean, when she was in her eighties, I would find her reading a newspaper. Pretty much up to her end, she subscribed to the *New York Times* and *The Washington Post*, as well as the local *Sentinel*. She clipped articles, usually from the inside pages, for future reference. I never quite understood what drew her to a specific article, but she told me, 'Little details offer big clues.' I guess that's why she usually could finish the *New York Times* crossword puzzle each week."

More details for my Amelia file, Callie thought.

"In regards to family pictures, you girls might want to check up in the attic," Mrs. Hodges said. "I haven't been up there in years, but I know it is full of trunks and such. It's a dusty mess up there, but you might find something useful."

"That's a great idea," Callie said.

Madison chimed in. "Wow, *'The Secret in the Old Attic'* was my favorite Nancy Drew Book!"

Twenty-eight

Well, it's about time someone came up with that suggestion, Tom thought. He floated into the attic when Callie opened the door. He was on a mission, focused on finding one specific item. *Where is it?* he asked himself as he moved around the edges of the room, trying not to stir up dust.

Unaware of Tom's invisible presence, Callie and Madison entered the dusty attic. The girls brushed cobwebs out of the way as they stepped into the large space. There was so much clutter that it took a moment for their eyes to focus on specific items. Against one wall, old mason jars and other glass items were stored on shelves. Beside the jars were six chairs with holes in their intricately woven cane seats. A walnut drop-leaf table leaned against another wall. One of its legs was broken, but it would be a beautiful piece if someone had the energy to refinish and repair it.

Callie's eyes were drawn to a collection of toys in the middle of the room. A hand-carved baby cradle was stored beside the toys. Callie put her hand on it and gently rocked it. She thought, *I wonder how many generations of Calafont babies slept in this cradle?* She noticed a box. When she opened it, she found a child's tea set. A few of the teacups were chipped. *Did Emily and Amelia have imaginary tea parties?* she wondered.

The spirit watched Callie pick up a small teacup. He was lost in memories of those long-ago tea parties, but he quickly refocused on his task at hand. *I do not have time to take a sentimental journey. I need to find it before the girls go back downstairs.*

Madison was not paying any attention to her friend. Her eyes were drawn to a stained-glass lamp shade on a shelf. "I bet this lampshade was made by Tiffany. I've seen pictures of them—they can be worth a fortune!" she said to no one. The shade lost her interest when she spotted some vintage clothes in a closet along one of the walls. On the top shelf were some old women's hats. She pulled out a straw one with a wide sash. She put it on her head and played with the sash until she had a perfect bow tied under her chin.

"What do you think of this one?" Madison said as she danced around and sang "I feel pretty."

They both knew the song from the musical *West Side Story*. Last year, Ada Lovelace joined with another private academy to produce the musical. Megan played Maria. Every time Megan came into the room, her friends teased her by singing the song.

Callie laughed. "That song is not appropriate. You look like you should be playing croquet at a lawn party instead of dancing with the Jets and the Sharks!"

Callie selected a wide-brim purple hat and put it on her head. "I think I saw this in the movie *Titanic*." She pulled down a feather boa, shook off its dust, and put it around her shoulder.

"Well, you don't look like Rose," Madison said, referring to the heroine of her favorite movie.

Callie reluctantly remembered their purpose. "Come on. We came up here to look for clues for our war room. Help me open this trunk."

In the meantime, Tom was busy looking in the nooks and crannies. He finally spotted what he was seeking underneath one of the dormer windows. He blew off the dust that covered it. *Now, where can I put this so that my two girls will find it?* He moved it to the floor, right beside the trunks.

Madison sneezed as they lifted the lid of the first trunk. There were no papers or photos in it, just some men's clothes and old boots.

The girls moved to the next trunk. It contained moth-eaten old blankets. Callie stepped back and practically tripped over something on the floor.

That's funny. I don't remember seeing this before, she thought as she bent down to examine what caused her to trip. It looked like a leather bag of some kind.

"Madison, look at this," Callie said, looking at the embossed initials on the bag. "Do these initials read C.S.A.? Do you think that means Confederate States of America?"

"I think you're right," Madison said. "I bet this was a knapsack."

It hit Callie and Madison at the same time, and they jointly said aloud, "Tom!"

"It's so dusty in here. Let's take this downstairs before we open it," Madison said as she sneezed again.

Tom relaxed. *Let's see what these two smart girls can do with the clues in my knapsack.* He followed them as they left the attic.

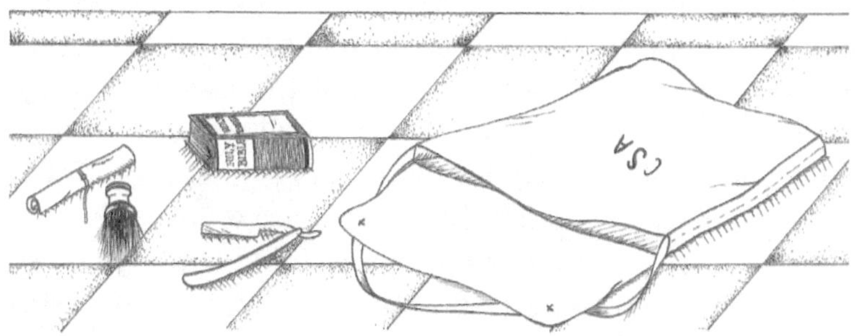

"What do you have there?" Mrs. Hodges asked as the girls carried the old and very dusty leather bag into the kitchen.

"We think it may have been Tom's knapsack. But we haven't opened it yet," Callie said.

"Well, don't put that dirty thing on my clean floor. Let me get you some newspapers to spread on the floor. You can open the bag on the papers." Mrs. Hodges industriously spread papers over the kitchen floor.

There were two bone buttons that kept the knapsack closed. Callie carefully unbuttoned them. Inside was a razor, a shaving brush, a worn Bible, and a folded leather pouch.

Tom watched as Callie laid out items from his life. He had carried the knapsack for three years, and each of these items held a memory. He remembered the afternoon Mattie gave him the razor. On that day in 1861, she reached out and stroked his cheek and said, "Tom, I don't care what the fashion is. I love the smooth feel of your soft cheek. Those whiskers that other men wear look like they scratch." So, Tom shaved his face every morning, even when the men around him grew beards.

Callie picked up the Bible first. It had been read frequently. She hoped that there would be some indication of ownership or information about the owner's family. There were marked passages, but Callie could find no information about the reader of those passages. Callie then opened the pouch. She found two wrinkled pieces of paper, obviously folded and unfolded many times. When Callie saw writing on them, she realized that she held two letters. It took a moment for her to make out the writing that had faded with time. She quietly read the two pages. She was still as she put down the second letter.

"What is it, Callie?" Madison asked.

Madison and Mrs. Hodges listened intently as Callie read the first letter aloud.

"October 1, 1862

My darling husband,

I hope this letter finds you safe. Bessie came by yesterday to share a letter from Hank. She said that the two of you are still watching over each other. It makes me sleep a little better knowing that you are with someone from home.

I have joyous news. We are going to have that baby we always wanted, probably sometime in April. If it is a boy, I want to name him Peter, after your father. I know that any son of yours will grow up to be a fine man. Of course, we will love a girl just as much if the Lord decides that is best.

Old man Watson came by with his young grandson to help with the tobacco. It looks like it will be a good crop. The neighbors sure have pitched in while you've been gone. I have been able to put aside enough for winter from the garden. We should be all right until you can come home.

I pray each day for your safe return and hope this war will be over soon.

Your loving wife,

Mattie"

"Isn't that sweet!" said Mrs. Hodges.

Madison looked at her friend closely. She did not understand the expression on Callie's face. This letter made you smile. Instead, Callie seemed sad.

"Callie, is something wrong?" Mad asked her friend.

"Listen to the second letter. It was written the following April," Callie said.

"April 20, 1863

Dear Brother,

You have a big healthy son. He is named Peter, just as Mattie wanted. For some reason that we are not meant to understand, the Lord took Mattie right after Peter was born. She just was not strong enough to survive his birth. I am glad that she got to hold your son and see her handsome boy.

We buried her in the family plot at Old Bethel Church, right next to your mother. Rev. McFarland said some nice words and read the 23rd Psalm. The neighbors all came out to say goodbye. Mattie was a good woman and we miss her. We took Peter home with us. We care for him just as we care for our Andrew.

We are both well, although John's hip does pain him at times. He says that he can still feel his right leg even though he no longer has it. He is sure that when it is cold in Fredericksburg, he feels the cold. He believes his missing leg is sending him messages from that field hospital where it was amputated. I always tell him that I would rather have a husband with one leg than no husband at all. I guess we are lucky. There have been so many men who will never come home, and I know that more will die before this war is over. We pray for your safe return.

It has been rainy here, but I was able to get some garden in the ground, so we should have enough food to get us through the winter.

John joins me in writing this letter.

Your loving brother and sister,

John and Sadie"

Tom was listening. When he heard Callie's voice reading Sadie's letter, he felt the pain. It felt just as sharp as it did the first time he read the letter. Then, it was a cold April night in Virginia, 1863. Now, more than a hundred fifty years later, he again felt tears on his cheek.

Callie also had tears on her cheeks. Her logical mind could not explain Tom's spirit; however, this knapsack proved that a solider named Tom once lived. He and Mattie loved each other. They lived in a world when women could and did die in childbirth. It all really happened to actual people a century and a half ago.

Callie had never thought much about the human cost of war. Now, she was living in a house where people had been directly impacted by two wars. It was not just Tom and Mattie's sad story; Amelia's life changed because of World War II. She lost Michael because of that war. She obviously never found a man to replace him, as she did not marry. Callie did not understand it all, but she knew that what had happened to these people directly affected her own life.

It was not until she came to the Calafont house that Callie thought much about America's Civil War. The novels that she previously read always treated that war in somewhat romantic terms. The suffering got lost. They often profiled determined and strong women who resolutely faced the challenges caused by the war. The men in their lives may have been gone, but the women overcame the problems with steadfast courage. Callie knew that it was never easy to move on after the men that you loved died.

When she was ten, she loved *Little Women*. Jo sold her hair, *her only pride*, so that her mother could visit Jo's father, who was in a military hospital in Washington., D.C. Callie had envied Jo's beautiful brown head of hair and thought she was so brave to cut it. Last year, Callie and Lee Anne watched *Gone with the Wind* on television. It seemed so dated. She had a difficult time with the stereotypes of African Americans and the romanticism of the Old South. She understood why Rhett tired of Scarlett's selfishness. All the death in the movie did not really make her sad. It all seemed to happen on the screen, not to real people. The only thing she really liked was looking at Scarlett's beautiful dresses.

This last week, Callie finished several of the books about the Battle of Gettysburg that she checked out of the library. The books described the violence and tragedy of those three days. Callie now thought about war in a new way. Callie knew what it meant to lose someone you loved deeply and how that loss changed your life. Nothing was the same after death. It was not the least bit romantic. It hurt. Tom, Mattie, Amelia, and Michael were once real people. They suffered just as she did.

She cried because she understood their pain.

Twenty-nine

The next morning, Callie and Madison updated Tom's board in their war room. They mined the letters for information—they found a lot. They now knew that Tom came from a state that grew tobacco. He had a good friend named Hank, whose wife was probably named Bessie. It appeared that Hank and Tom served in the same regiment. Tom's brother was named John and his sister-in-law was Sadie. John and Sadie's son was Andrew, and they raised Tom's son Peter. Tom's wife, Mattie, died in the spring of 1863. All of this information was written on yellow stickies and placed on Tom's board.

The phone rang just as they placed the last piece of data. Mrs. Hodges picked up the extension in the kitchen.

"Your mother is on the phone, Callie." Mrs. Hodges called to her.

Callie ran to pick up the phone.

"Callie, how's it going? Are you enjoying Pennsylvania?" Lee Anne asked immediately.

"Mom, you will not believe what I am discovering about Aunt Amelia. You know I look like her. I never knew where my red hair came from, but I must carry her genes. It is so neat to actually look like a relative!"

Lee Anne could hear the excitement in her daughter's voice. This summer was giving Callie something that she could not offer her: a connection to her father's family. Again, Lee Anne thought, *Thank you, Amelia. Not just for providing for our future, but for giving Callie back life's joy.*

"Mom, I'm so glad that you called. I miss you a lot, although so much has been happening. I cannot wait to show you our war room."

"Excuse me, did you say 'war room?'" Lee Anne gasped.

"Mom, relax. Think detective show on television. We are investigating two mysteries. We are trying to find out about Tom, the Confederate soldier, whose story is part of the lore of this house. Mom, we found his picture. He was *so* good looking. His wife was named Mattie and she was a really pretty blonde. Then we actually found his knapsack. The knapsack had two letters in it. Oh, it is so sad. Mattie died in childbirth while Tom was away fighting for the Confederacy."

Lee Anne was amazed at all the facts that her daughter had uncovered. "His actual knapsack? That is really something."

Then it hit Lee Anne what her daughter had said. "Did you say two mysteries? What is the other one?"

"I want to find out what Amelia did during World War II. She appears to be involved in something top secret. And, Mom, she was in love. His name was Michael. I think he must have died in the war. I found this note she wrote right before she died. It almost made me cry." Callie cited almost verbatim Amelia's note. "Aren't you curious, Mom? Don't you want to know about her *top-secret* work?"

"It is a bit of a mystery," Lee Anne said. "You know, Mark Hamilton may have some ideas about Amelia's life during that time. I think from what he has said, his father and Amelia knew each other when they were young."

"Can you ask him if he has seen any pictures of Amelia when she was a young woman? I would love to see Amelia when she was in her twenties. It will be like looking at me in the future. Kind of cool, don't you think?"

Lee Anne smiled at her daughter's excitement. "Well, I don't know if I would put it quite that way. The events of Amelia's life may have affected how she looked, but I can see why you are interested. I'm having some people over for dinner tonight, and Mark and Jackie will be here. I'll ask him then."

"Mom, I am so glad that you are making friends. I was a little worried that you were moving just because you thought that it was good for me to go to Ada Lovelace. You are happy, too, aren't you?" Callie queried, inquisitively.

"Callie, my new life is working out well," Lee Anne said reassuringly. "Yes, I can honestly say, 'I am happy.' We both owe a lot to Aunt Amelia. I'll talk with you soon. Give my love to both Madison and Mrs. Hodges."

Thirty

Washington, D.C.

June 2013

Lee Anne was very pleased with her first party in her new home. Compared to Jackie Hamilton's well-known dinner parties, it was a small gathering, only twelve guests, but everyone seemed to have a good time. Her closest friends, Bob McPherson and Jackie and Mark Hamilton, stayed after the others left. Lee Anne topped off their wine glasses and sat down to join them.

"It was a wonderful evening," Jackie said. "Now, let me pour you a glass of wine. Just relax and tell us about Callie's adventures in Pennsylvania. You said that you talked to her today."

"She is having a wonderful time so far," Lee Anne said. "I am so grateful to Aunt Amelia. She has made such a difference in Callie. She is no longer grieving her father's death, but appreciates the legacy that he has left her. Callie is even identifying with Amelia Calafont. Apparently, Callie looks *very* much like her."

"I thought that myself the first time I met Callie," Mark interjected.

"Mark, that reminds me," Lee Anne said. "Callie is very interested in Amelia's life when she was in her twenties, during World War II. She cannot find any pictures of Amelia from that period. I am under the impression that your father knew her during that time. I told Callie I would ask you if you knew anything about Amelia's life then."

"I don't know anything specific, except that Amelia and my father, Bill Hamilton, were friends during the war years," Mark said. "He was a naval officer. He spent the last days of the war on a battleship in the Pacific, but he was stationed in D.C. before he deployed. I was always under the impression that he and Amelia dated during that time. I would also like to know more about Dad's life then. I wish I could talk to him about it, but you know he has been gone for almost five years." Mark was lost in his own thoughts about his father.

Bob drew the conversation back to Callie. "Has she had any supernatural encounters? I'm not sure that I believe all the strange occurrences in the house are caused by the spirit of a Confederate soldier, but I do know that unexplainable things happen there."

"As a matter of fact, Callie and Madison found evidence that a Confederate soldier named Tom was in the house at one time. They found his knapsack in the attic," Lee Anne said.

"Really, his actual knapsack? That I would love to see!" Mark said.

"Callie is convinced that he was in a Confederate regiment that came north during the Gettysburg campaign, probably one that marched in front of the Calafont house. She has an idea that if she can identify these regiments, she may be able to identify his last name. You know how smart she is. She is being very systematic about her research efforts."

"She may be onto something there. I know that the National Park Service has done a lot of work to digitize the names of the soldiers in the regiments that fought at Gettysburg. It may actually be possible for her to find some leads to our Tom," Mark offered.

He thought for a moment. "I may even be able to help get her to the information she needs. Ryan Nelson is a good friend. You remember him, Jackie. He and his wife, Beth, came to our Christmas party."

"Of course," Jackie said. "I really like them a lot. How do you think he can help Callie?"

"He holds some sort of executive position at the Department of the Interior. His branch oversees the National Park Service. I'll give him a call tomorrow and see if he can connect Callie with the right person to get her the information she needs. Ryan knows how to cut bureaucratic red tape. He is very good at it. It may be much faster than going through channels." Mark said.

Lee Anne just marveled. She was living in a different world now. Mark and Jackie Hamilton opened doors.

Thirty-one

The Limestone House

June 2013

A few days later, Callie received a phone call from Gordon Hall, the head of the research department at the Gettysburg National Battlefield. Callie liked the sound of his voice. He sounded like one of her favorite teachers.

After introducing himself, Mr. Hall quickly got to the point of his call. "I understand you are searching for a soldier who was part of the Confederate forces in Pennsylvania during the Gettysburg campaign."

She could not believe that he knew she was researching Tom's story. "Wow," said Callie, "How do you know this?"

"You have friends in some high places. Perhaps I can help you if you tell me what you already know."

Callie had no idea who he meant in terms of her friends, but it was exciting to share the facts she knew about Tom with him. While she talked, she was careful not to describe Tom as a ghost. She wanted Mr. Hall to take her research seriously.

"My ancestors lived in a limestone house on Walnut Bottom Road, close to Carlisle. There are family stories about a Confederate soldier named Tom, no last name, only his first name. A few weeks ago, we found his knapsack in the attic. There were some letters in it that offer clues to his identity. We would love to find out as much as we can about him."

"His actual knapsack? That *is* a find," Mr. Hall said. "Off the top of my head, I believe that Ramseur's Brigade marched down Walnut Bottom Road, but I would have to check for sure. We might be able to offer some clues to your mystery. Can you come to Gettysburg and I can arrange for you to meet with my staff?"

"That would be great!" Callie said, excited by the invitation. "Can I bring a friend with me? We can come down next week."

"Absolutely, bring your friend. Next Wednesday would be best. We are always very crowded on weekends during the summer; however, this year, as we approach the one hundred fiftieth anniversary of the battle, the traffic is worse than ever. By the way, are either of you really good with computers? Our records are now digitized, but even so, there are thousands of potential candidates for your Tom. I think somebody who knows how to manipulate computer files could speed up the process. Unfortunately, my best IT expert is out on emergency medical leave. I do not expect him back for several weeks, and it sounds as if you are eager to find some answers."

"Computer expertise I can probably provide!" Callie said. "I know just the right person. We will see you next Wednesday around 10 a.m.," Callie said.

"I look forward to it," Mr. Hall said as he hung up the phone.

Callie turned to Madison, who had been listening in on the conversation.

"Mad, we just have to get Aimee up here. In our last text, she was still at her parent's house in Frederick. That's not very far away. Let's text her right now."

Mad pulled out her phone and sent off a text to Aimee.

Aimee texted back immediately. "Sounds like fun! Boring here. I'll see if I can drive up next Tuesday for the week."

Callie went off to find Mrs. Hodges and prepare her for another guest. There was no doubt in either Callie or Mad's minds that Aimee would arrive on Tuesday. They both knew that she could talk her parents into anything.

Aimee was an only child, and her parents doted on her. Her father was originally from Nigeria. He left his homeland in his twenties to study international finance at Cambridge. Aimee's father was committed to the people of the developing world and knew that it was important that these countries understand the world of finance. There he met Aimee's mother, a blonde English woman with a peaches and cream complexion. Aimee inherited the best physical features from both her parents. Her skin was as flawless as her mother's, but its tone was light brown. She had her father's big brown eyes, with long eyelashes that curled naturally. When you looked at her, you first noticed those eyes, but you then discovered that she had a brilliant mind. She was able to calculate most math problems in her head, but she loved making a computer do the calculations even faster.

The following Tuesday, right on schedule, at two o'clock, Aimee's car pulled into the Calafont driveway. Callie ran to the front door to greet her. To her surprise, Aimee was not alone.

"Megan, you're here, too!" Callie shouted in pleasure.

"Of course, I'm here. Did you think that I was going to let you three have all the fun this summer?" Megan said, laughing.

Thirty-two

"Now, what is all of this about ghosts and a World War II love story," Megan asked.

"I think it will be easiest to explain it all by visiting our war room," Callie said.

Callie and Mad led the two newcomers to the sunroom with the two large boards devoted to Tom and Amelia. Mad took over and explained what they knew about both. The girls read the letters that they found in Tom's knapsack and Amelia's last note.

Megan was visibly moved by the words written so many years ago. "How incredibly sad," she said.

Like Callie, Megan understood the personal loss felt by both Tom and Amelia. But when Callie told of her conversation with Mr. Hall and the planned visit to Gettysburg the next day, their friend Aimee became engaged.

Aimee stood back and looked at Tom's board. She had brought her laptop with her, loaded with several tools that she could use to mine the data. She was eager to start working on her computer program. She was already planning the logic in her head. She knew that if the data was there, she had the ability to slice and dice it.

Megan was drawn to Amelia's story. The other three always teased her that she was "the born romantic in the group." She loved reading Jane Austen and anything by one of the Bronte' sisters. *Wuthering Heights* was her favorite book. Megan did not know if it was because of her national inclination toward romance or because Amelia loved music as she did, but regardless of the reason, she wanted to know more about Amelia. She looked at her good friend Callie, but instead of seeing a sixteen-year old girl in the twenty-first century, she now saw Amelia Calafont in World War II vintage clothes.

While Aimee was busy planning their approach to unraveling Tom's story, Megan had no clue how to proceed in finding out about Amelia; however, she felt that it was important that they do so. After all, it was Amelia who had changed her good friend's life.

While the other three girls were busy talking about the next day's trip to Gettysburg, Megan wandered into the parlor and sat down at the piano. She could not resist putting her hands on the keyboard. She played the classical piece by Chopin that she memorized for the spring recital at Ada Lovelace. That night she had worn a lacy black dress, and her hair hung down her back in curls. Although she was now dressed in shorts and her hair was in a pony tail, she managed to look very feminine as she played the notes. She always came into her own when she was playing music.

After she played the last note, she looked around for something else to play. She knew that most people kept music under the seat of their piano bench. Sure enough, Amelia had followed that tradition. There were several large music books full of pieces to develop skills. None of these particularly attracted Megan. She was not in the mood for that type of practice.

Megan noticed a yellow envelope underneath the books. She pulled it out. Stamped on it was a return address of a music store on Fifth Avenue in New York City. She looked inside and pulled out a piece of sheet music for the popular love song from the 1940s, "I'll Be Seeing You."

Oh, I know this song, she thought. She began to hum the tune. Last year, the Ada Lovelace's choral group had sung a medley of World War II songs for the residents of a local retirement village. The senior citizens loved the afternoon, and they offered the girls tea and scones. This song was Megan's personal favorite from the medley. As she read the pretty lyrics, she could picture the song's familiar places: the café, the park, the children's carousel. She put the music on the piano

and began playing the notes. Soon she was singing the words.

Drawn by the beautiful melody, Callie, Madison, and Aimee left the war room and surrounded the piano.

"That is so pretty, Megan. Where did you find that song?" Callie asked.

"It was in this envelope, underneath all the song books. I hope it was all right that I looked through the music."

Callie took the envelope. She realized that there was a piece of paper inside it. She pulled it out.

"Look, it's a letter from Michael to Amelia."

The other three listened as Callie read aloud.

September 20, 1944

My Dearest Darling,

Amelia, I cannot say goodbye. We will never say goodbye.

This night must be our last night together for a while. We knew this day would come. I have been stationed at the Pentagon for long enough. My re-assignment has come through. I must rejoin the fight.

I leave you this song. Its words describe my feelings better than I can do. I first saw you playing the piano at Arlington Farms. I think I fell in love just watching you that night. You were the center of the group, your fingers making music for us all.

I must leave our familiar places. But wherever I am, I will be seeing you. It will be easy, because I will carry you with me in my heart.

I will love you forever,

Michael

"How romantic," Megan said with a sigh.

"I wonder what Arlington Farms was?" Aimee said.

Aimee had noticed the reference in Michael's letter. Ada Lovelace was not too far from Arlington, but she had never heard of such a location. Arlington was a suburb of Washington, D.C., and there definitely were no farms there.

"I've got this covered," Madison proclaimed. She had already pulled out her phone and did a search for Arlington Farms.

"Here it is," she announced. "Listen to this. Arlington Farms was a women's dorm during World War II. Apparently, thousands of young women lived there who came to work for the government during the war. The buildings are no longer there and the land is now part of Arlington Cemetery. It looks like it was a really cool place to live. There was even maid service. It was modeled on college dorms and there were pianos in the lounges. Look at these pictures of girls openly kissing soldiers. And our parents complain about *our* generation!"

The girls passed around Mad's phone and looked at the photos posted on the internet. In addition to pictures of girls locked in passionate embraces with G.I.s, there was a picture of girls and soldiers gathered around a piano.

"Just think, Amelia could have played that piano," Megan said.

Thirty-three

The Limestone House

December 1945

Tom listened to the raven-haired girl play Amelia's song. Her voice turned the words into a beautiful melody. However, when Amelia played the song during those first months of 1946, it sounded so mournful. He remembered that painful time as if it were yesterday.

Amelia came home in December of 1945. She never left again. Anna Calafont was wrapped up with the preparations for the wedding of her younger daughter Emily. She did not have time to absorb the sadness in her oldest daughter's eyes. Amelia tried to join the celebratory mood of the Calafont house. There were Christmas decorations everywhere. She attended what seemed to be an endless number of bridal showers for Emily and had fittings for her maid of honor dress. She did a pretty good job of hiding her feelings, but Tom saw beneath her forced smile. He recognized the signs of grief.

It was a very traditional wedding. On Saturday, the twenty-second day of December, Emily floated gracefully down the wide Calafont staircase. She wore her mother's wedding dress and Robert gave his younger daughter's hand to a man he barely knew. The entire neighborhood attended the nuptials. Everyone was in a jubilant mood. The war was over, the soldiers, sailors, and airmen were home, and everyone seemed to be getting married. The guests did not really understand why the bride did not follow the local tradition of tossing her bouquet to her maid of honor. Everyone expected that Amelia would catch it. Surely, she would follow in her younger sister's footsteps and walk down the aisle. Emily knew the sad truth. Her sister had shared with her that Michael was not coming home. He had been killed, someplace on the other side of the Rhine. His death seemed so unfair—he died just a few days before V-E day and Germany's surrender—so Emily decided not to toss her bouquet, a small thing to help protect Amelia from further anguish.

The guests threw rice at the happy couple. Amelia hugged Emily and pushed back her tears as she said goodbye. The newlyweds headed off for their new life in Kansas. It was that night, after all the guests left, that Amelia first played "I'll Be Seeing You."

During the first months of 1946, it did not worry Tom that Amelia played this tune. It was a way for her to express her feelings. But by April, he began to worry. She was not able to move beyond the intense first stages of grief. Her mood seemed to be getting worse. Every night she sat in the parlor and played the song again. She no longer needed the sheet music Michael had sent her. She knew the song by heart.

Tom tried to comfort her but he was at a loss. He had no idea how to help her move forward. Surprisingly, it was not the spirit who gave Amelia an interest in life again but her father, Robert Calafont. Robert was also worried. His once energetic and inquisitive daughter was lethargic. In his own way, Robert loved her very much, but he had no experience in dealing with someone in such a delicate emotional state. In fact, Robert did not even acknowledge that he himself had any emotions. It was over breakfast on a May morning in 1946 that Robert connected with Amelia. He was reading the *Wall Street Journal* over his coffee. It was his daily ritual. He always checked the stock market activity of the previous day before he headed off to his office at Cumberland Mutual Trust. Like many businessmen, Robert did not trust the current administration in Washington. He was really not sure if President Truman was up to the task. After all, the man from Missouri had failed as a businessman. He was worried that post-war spending was heading the country into an inflationary spiral. His mind was on these issues, and he was really not paying any attention to his oldest daughter.

Amelia was up earlier than usual that morning. She poured a cup of tea, buttered a piece of toast, and joined her father at the breakfast table. Her eyes landed on the stock reports as he turned the page. It was then that Amelia shocked her father. She asked him about the Dow Jones Industrial Averages. None of the women in his family had ever shown any interest in business issues. He explained to her the column headers and how to interpret the numbers. When he left for work, Amelia picked up the paper and began to study the data. The next morning, she asked her father additional questions. He answered them.

As they talked, Robert Calafont was amazed. His daughter's observations were very astute. From that morning forward, Robert and Amelia Calafont talked about business trends over coffee before Robert left for work. She was soon offering her father investment advice. It was not long before he realized that he would be very wise to take it.

Robert Calafont did not know that his daughter was using skills that just a year earlier had helped America win the war in the Pacific. Then, she recognized trends and patterns regarding Japanese ship movements. They were the same skills that she now applied to analyzing the daily stock market. She read everything she could about national and world events. She predicted how they would affect stock prices. She was usually right.

One night in early August, as the summer of 1946 drew to a close, Amelia sat on her bed and looked through a box of her mementoes from the war years. There was her recruitment letter from January of 1942. She had no idea what she was being recruited to do, but the letter made it sound important. During the interview she was only asked whether she liked to solve puzzles. It was an easy question. She had spent many hours with her grandfather, Matthew, working on crossword puzzles in his library. She gave the right answer and was told to report to Arlington Hall.

Amelia looked at a photo of the building where she had worked for almost four years. In her mind, she saw her desk inside the building and pages of coded numbers from Japanese transmissions that needed to be deciphered. There were several pictures of women. They worked together in close proximity to decode the enemy plans. They all lived together at Arlington Farms. Amelia remembered their fun nights. She read again her commendation letter, thanking her for her valuable service, but with strict instructions to keep her work secret. If she was ever asked what she did during the war, she was told to tell people that she just sharpened pencils and emptied trash.

She found the picture she was seeking. It was of a tall man in a major's uniform. She looked at his face for a long time. As always, it was Michael's eyes that she noticed. Even in the black and white photo, she could see laughter in them. She did not open the envelope that Colonel Donovan hand-delivered to her after the end of the war. She could not read that letter again. She knew its contents.

Amelia opened a leather-bound book. Emily had given her the journal when she left for Washington and told her to write of her adventures. The first pages were filled with descriptions of the crowded city, but many of the pages remained blank. There was too much happening during those years for Amelia to take the time to write about her life. She opened a blank page and picked up a pen. She wrote with pride that she had been part of the war effort, but she did not write any details about her work. She had been sworn to secrecy. It was an oath that she intended to take to her grave. She wrote of her friends and their fun times. Then, with a smile on her lips, she wrote of Michael, not the sadness of his death, but of their long talks, his sense of humor, and his intelligence.

She wrote of the feel of her hand in his hand and the softness of his lips on hers. It was late in the night when she closed the journal and put down her pen.

Amelia looked around her room. She saw the chest of drawers that the first Pennsylvanian Calafont gave to his bride. She had discovered its secret when she was fourteen. There was a bump on the side of the bottom drawer. She pressed it now and a hidden compartment opened. She placed the photos, letters, and the journal inside. She closed the compartment that now held her memories.

That fall she began teaching children at the local elementary school. She loved them. But every morning, she and her father talked about business trends, productivity statements, and balance sheets.

She never again played 'I'll Be Seeing You.'

Thirty-four

Gettysburg, PA

June 2013

Callie, Madison, Aimee, and Megan pulled out of the Calafont driveway early the next morning. Callie was impatient to get going. It had taken forever for all four girls to get out the door. Callie remembered her Grandpa Matt's expression "herding cats." It certainly applied to her friends. Just when she thought they were all ready, Mad ran back to the kitchen to grab another one of Mrs. Hodges' blueberry muffins.

Callie relaxed as Aimee finally turned her car to head down Walnut Bottom Road. Callie, riding shotgun, gave her directions. One hundred and fifty years earlier, Confederate soldiers marched down this road as they left Calafont land. It was a dirt road then, with deep wagon ruts. Now it was two lanes, paved with asphalt, but the path the Southerners took that day was the same one that the four girls were taking in Aimee's car. On her lap, she held Tom's knapsack. She had placed the letters back in the pouch and returned all the items to the bag. The dust was now gone but, otherwise, the knapsack was exactly as she found it. She hoped that Mr. Hall might see some details about Tom that she had missed.

Madison may have been in the backseat, but that did not mean that she was silent. Mad was never silent for very long. Everything was an adventure for her, and she always enjoyed a good road trip; however, she never drove aimlessly. She always wanted to know where she was going and why she was going there. Madison had to have a goal. It was what drove her on the basketball court or the soccer field. She opened her phone and typed *Gettysburg* into her search engine. She found the articles she was seeking and began to read aloud about the battle that changed the course of the American Civil War.

"Mad, you sound like a guide on a tourist bus," Callie teased.

Madison stuck her tongue out at Callie but continued reading. Not used to citing large numbers aloud, she stumbled over figures as she read, "165,620 combined Union and Confederate forces, 93,921 fighting for the Union and 71,699 for the Confederates, fought in the Battle."

The girls were quiet after Madison read her final statistics.

"Some accounts estimate that over 58,000 men, 31,000 from the Union and 27,000 from the South, died in just three days," Madison said as she finished reading the statistics.

Aimee focused on her driving, but the numbers penetrated her subconsciousness. She liked dealing with numbers. She understood them. Her computers gave her the power to manipulate them and make them work for her. It was people she always had a difficult time understanding. She was often surprised by the reaction of those she met. She realized that her world travels, appearance, and clothes gave her an air of sophistication, but in reality, Aimee had led a very sheltered life. Her parents and both sets of grandparents, one British and the other Nigerian, protected her from the evil and violence in the world. People who judged others solely based on appearance or skin color were new to her. Numbers did not have such problems. Numbers were factual, not judgmental. However, the numbers that Mad read aloud did not represent abstract ideas. Each one represented a person. It was hard for Aimee to wrap her head around that many people dying.

Megan also was moved by Madison's recitation of the bloody battle. As they drove through the Pennsylvania countryside, she looked out the window as she listened to Madison read. The rural scenery was beautiful. She pictured soldiers wearing uniforms marching through the land. She heard Madison tell of places that were part of American history, such as the Peach Orchard, Seminary Ridge, Devil's Den, and Little Roundtop. The names sounded poetic to her. She closed her eyes. There was nothing poetic or the least bit romantic about thousands of men losing their lives at those pretty sounding places.

Callie did not listen to the details that Madison read. She had spent the last month immersed in the Battle of Gettysburg. Now, as Aimee's car drew closer to the sight of so much bloodshed, Callie's thoughts were not on the monumental battle but on the immediate days before the two armies met. She was convinced that it was then that Tom's spirit found a home in the Calafont house. She believed that Tom was in a Confederate regiment that fought at Gettysburg, but Callie was sure that he died before the big battle. He must have died on Calafont land. It was the only thing that made sense. If he actually died in the battle, his knapsack would not be in the attic; it would have been left on a field thirty miles away. It was logical, and Callie always tried to apply logic to any situation.

It was after ten when Aimee pulled into the already crowded parking lot at the Gettysburg National Military Park. She finally found a parking space in the last row, a long way from the visitor center. It was already a hot June day, and the air-conditioned center felt almost cold when the girls pushed open its glass doors. Callie looked at the clock on the wall. She was relieved. It was only 10:10. She always hated being late, but they had plenty of time. They were scheduled to meet Mr. Hall at 10:30.

There was a long line of people at the information desk. While Callie waited her turn, she watched two little boys run around with blue Union caps on their heads. Their mother did not even try to calm them. Callie imagined that they had been cooped up in the car for hours and they needed to work off their energy. She looked at her friends. She thought Madison must have been like the boys when she was their age. Madison never sat still for very long, and even now, at seventeen, she was fidgety after the long drive. When Callie reached the front of the line, she told the park ranger that she had an appointment with Gordon Hall. She could tell that the ranger was impressed. He immediately picked up the phone and placed a call.

A few minutes later, Callie watched a middle-aged man with salt and pepper hair approach her. She knew instantly that he was Mr. Hall. He walked through the crowd with an air of authority. Callie remembered that he had sounded like one of her favorite teachers on the phone, and his appearance matched his warm voice.

"Hello, you must be Callie Monroe, and I assume these are your friends. I am Gordon Hall."

Callie liked him immediately. He shook her hand, a good sign that he was not going to treat her like a bothersome teenager. She introduced him to her three friends.

"I've arranged for us to meet with one of my best researchers. He is an expert on the invasion of the North by the Confederates. He is very knowledgeable about the Southern command structure and troop movements. He's waiting for us in one of the conference rooms."

Thirty-five

Jason Andrews stood when the park director walked into the conference room with the four girls. His mouth almost dropped open. When Mr. Hall told him that they were meeting with someone who had political connections in Washington, D.C., he had pictured someone older, maybe a middle-aged woman searching for her ancestors. The last thing that he expected was that the "politically connected person" would be four girls, ten years younger than he was.

Mr. Hall handled the introductions. "Jason is as knowledgeable as anyone about Confederate regiments. He is working on his doctoral dissertation and is taking a bit of a break from academia to give us a hand this summer."

Callie looked at the tall, thin young man with thick glasses. She was not surprised that he was a doctoral candidate. He looked as if he had spent most of his life among library stacks.

Mr. Hall continued, "Jason, Callie has a mystery she

would like us to help her solve. Callie, why don't you bring Jason up to speed."

"My family home is located on Walnut Bottom Road, close to Carlisle. There is a family story about a Confederate soldier named Tom, who has connections to the house," Callie began.

As she talked, Callie intentionally avoided the words ghost or spirit. "About a week ago, we found a knapsack in the attic. We think it belonged to this soldier. We want to find out anything we can about him."

"You found his actual knapsack?" Jason interjected.

"Yes, we brought it along. We also have his picture that was on display with other family photos," Callie said as she laid the leather knapsack and daguerreotype of Tom and Mattie on the table.

Both Mr. Hall and Jason moved to the table for a closer look.

"Is it all right if I open it?" Jason asked.

The excitement in the young scholar's voice was obvious.

"Of course," Callie said.

Jason put on white gloves and unfastened the bone button, opened the knapsack, and laid the items, one by one, almost reverently, on the table.

We sure were casual with how we handled what Jason would call historic artifacts, Callie thought.

"I see the name Tom on the back of the photo. Do you have other information?" Jason asked.

"In the leather pouch, there is a letter from his wife, Mattie—she's the blonde in the photo—and another one from his sister-in-law," Callie said.

Jason carefully opened the letters, read them, and looked at the daguerreotype closely.

"Confederate soldiers frequently carried a knapsack like this one. It contained their prized possessions, and it is likely that it only left a soldier's side when he died. I have seen such knapsacks in our collection, but none in this condition. Most of the ones I have seen were found on the battlefield after the battle."

As he continued to study the knapsack, Jason said, "I would be very surprised if Tom died on our battlefield or, for that matter, in any other Civil War battle. This knapsack's condition is much too pristine. Civil War battles were very bloody affairs. The description of Gettysburg after the battle is especially horrific. Dead bodies everywhere. Officially, we now say 41,000 men died here, but previous accounts were as high as 58,000, and I'm inclined to believe that the number is really closer to the high end. Civil War musket balls left dead bodies that were particularly bloody, with body parts and gore spilling out. More than 5,000 horses were also killed in the battle, and their dead bodies added to the carnage."

Megan shivered as she pictured the scene Jason described. "How awful," she exclaimed.

Jason paused and said again, "No, I do not think the

soldier who carried this knapsack died in battle. But that is not too surprising. Thousands of men died during the war of diseases, some of which we understand today to be measles or dysentery. Some died of heat stroke on their long marches, but others died of something they called camp fever. We are not really sure what that means in today's medical parlance."

Jason opened a page to a map showing red and blue lines, indicating the movement of the armies. The red line indicated rebel troop movements and the blue line represented the Northern army.

"Where did you say you found this knapsack?" he asked. "In a house on Walnut Bottom Road? Can you show me on the map?"

Callie pointed out the location of the limestone house on the map. It was clear that the red line went right through Calafont land.

At that point, Madison joined the conversation.

"We think that Tom may have been in a regiment in Ramseur's Brigade," Madison said.

Jason looked at her, impressed. These girls had done their homework.

"That's very possible," Jason said. "This line represents the movement of Rodes' Division. He was one of Ewell's generals. Ewell reported directly to Robert E. Lee. Rodes' Division was made up of Daniel, Iverson, and Ramseur's Brigades. Confederate troops entered Carlisle from the west. The goal of these troops was to take the capitol city of Harrisburg, and they moved through the Cumberland Valley quickly toward that goal. They never made it to Harrisburg because Lee called them to Gettysburg."

"See, Tom could very likely have been in that Brigade," Madison exclaimed.

"Do you think it is possible to prove this by finding the names of the people who fought with Ramseur?" Callie asked.

"Well, perhaps," Jason said." It's a lot easier to track members of Union regiments and what happened to them than Confederate regiments. We really do not have complete information on all the individual Confederate soldiers who died during the Gettysburg Campaign. The dead Union soldiers were buried and then later rein-terred in the Gettysburg National Cemetery. Remember, Lincoln came to Gettysburg to dedicate this cemetery and deliver his famous address. The victors did not pay as much attention to the enemy dead. Some Confeder-ates were buried in mass graves, and no record of the individual Southern soldiers in these graves were kept. However, over the years, historians have made their best efforts to compile the names of these soldiers and their regiments. Recently, the National Park Service has gone further and digitized this information."

Jason continued, "Since I understood from Mr. Hall that you were looking for a specific individual soldier, I copied data to a thumb drive for you. There are over 71,000 Confederate soldiers listed on it with their regi-ments. It's a large file. I am not a computer expert, so I made no attempt to organize it."

"This is where I come in," Aimee said, stepping forward. "Can I see the thumb drive?"

She opened her laptop and inserted the small thumb drive into her USB port and pressed a few keys. A list of names and other data quickly scrolled passed them on the screen.

"I can work with this. It should be easy to dump this into a database, and then we can search for our Tom. Right now, I am just going to copy the file onto my laptop as a backup to the thumb drive."

Jason was always in awe of people who easily used technology. Aimee clearly knew what she was doing.

Callie realized that Aimee was probably excited to get started, but the battlefield was one of the major historic sites in America. It would be a shame not to see more of the park before they left, and Mr. Hall's next words echoed her thought.

"I'm very glad that we might have been able to help you today, but I would hate for you to leave without experiencing Gettysburg. One of the best ways to do so is to see our cyclorama."

"What's a cyclorama?" Megan asked.

"Cycloramas were a very popular form of entertainment in the late 1800s, both in America and in Europe," Mr. Hall said. "They were massive oil paintings that recreated historic events. People stood on a platform and felt like they were actually at the event. As an entertainment form, cycloramas died out with the introduction of motion pictures. The Battle of Gettysburg cyclorama is one of a few that has survived. It has been restored, but the original painting was finished in 1883. The artist who painted it based his depiction on interviews with actual survivors of the battle. I find it a more personal way to experience the battle than a modern movie."

"We'd love to see it," Callie said.

Mr. Hall led the four girls through a special door reserved for staff. Once inside, the cyclorama experience soon started, with sound effects and lights that brought the battle to life. The painting featured the third day of battle, when Robert E. Lee ordered General Pickett's forces across an open field to charge the Union forces. Union artillery mowed the Southerners down.

The girls were silent when the show was over. Again, they were struck by the magnitude of the battle and the sheer number of people who died during it.

Afterwards, Mr. Hall treated the girls to lunch in the cafeteria.

The girls thanked him profusely for lunch and all his help. They knew that they had taken up enough of his time, so they said their good-byes, but before leaving, they took him up on his suggestion to visit the museum and bookstore. They treated themselves to some fudge, to sustain them on the ride home, and they bought a scarf for Mrs. Hodges.

It was late in the afternoon when the four tired girls made their way back to the car. It had been a long day, and even the usual talkative Madison was quiet on the way home.

Thirty-six

The Limestone House

June 26, 2013

The morning after their trip to the Gettysburg Military Park, Aimee set up her work area in the war room. She placed her laptop on a table and arranged her space. An organized workspace was very important to her. She first created her database structure to match Jason's file. She then loaded the data from the thumb drive into this new structure.

Callie, Madison, and Megan surrounded her as she worked. Aimee knew that she might not find their Tom and tried to prepare her friends for this reality.

"Don't worry, Aimee, we won't take it out on you if you can't find Tom," Callie said in a comforting tone. "We know we're looking for a needle in a haystack."

"Well, computers can find needles, or as my father likes to say, 'separate the wheat from the chaff,'" Aimee said.

Once she had the database established, she was ready to begin.

"Now, let's enter some search criteria. Our first goal is to create a smaller universe, or to use Callie's expression, a smaller haystack, and 71,699 entries are far too many. Unfortunately, I cannot go directly to Ramseur's Brigade. The data is not arranged that way," Aimee said. "Madison, didn't you find information on the net that listed the regiments in his brigade? Maybe we can start there."

"Yes, here they are," Madison said as she retrieved the information from the internet. "There are only four regiments, and they are all from North Carolina: the 2nd, 4th, 14th, and 30th."

Megan came alive. "Didn't Mattie mention their tobacco crop in her letter? Last year, we went to the Outer Banks on vacation, and we passed through lots of tobacco farms in North Carolina. It makes sense that Mattie and Tom would have lived there."

Aimee created a smaller file that only contained information on soldiers who had served in these regiments.

"This is much better," she said. "We now have only 1,030 possible candidates. Let's go for broke and look for Tom among these entries."

Callie cautioned her, "Make sure that you look for Tom, Thomas, or Tommy, and you better look for Tom in both the first and middle names."

"Good idea," said Aimee, and she entered in a new search request.

The computer responded. The girls stared at the screen. There were only sixteen people that met the new criteria:

> Thomas Miller, Private, 14th N.C. Regiment
> Michael Thomas Christianson, Sergeant, 2nd N.C. Regiment
> Tommy Jackson, Private, 30th N.C. Regiment
> Thomas McDonald, Private, 14th N.C. Regiment
> Thomas Baker, Corporal, 2nd N.C. Regiment
> John Thomas Stephens, Private, 30th N.C. Regiment
> Thomas McGuire, Private, 2nd N.C. Regiment
> Thomas Donaldson, Private, 30th N.C. Regiment
> Thomas Nelson, Private, 14th N.C. Regiment
> Thomas Johnson, Private, 4th N.C. Regiment
> Thomas Russell, Sergeant, 4th N.C. Regiment
> Thomas Hancock, Private, 2nd N.C. Regiment
> Thomas Miller, Lieutenant, 14th N.C. Regiment
> Tom Coleman, Corporal, 30th N.C. Regiment
> Thomas Fraser, Corporal, 4th N.C. Regiment
> Thomas Rankine, Private, 2nd N.C. Regiment

"Wow!" Madison exclaimed. "Just think, one of these men is probably with us right now."

"But which one?" Aimee said. "I have no idea how to drill down further."

The girls looked hopelessly at each other. They might be close, but still they had no idea of Tom's actual identity. No one could think of any way around this roadblock.

They had not paid any attention to the time as they worked. They were surprised when Mrs. Hodges called them to lunch.

"Well, we might as well eat. Food never hurts!" Madison said.

As the girls enjoyed the grilled cheese sandwiches Mrs. Hodges had made, Megan was especially complimentary.

"These are *so* good, Mrs. Hodges! My grandmother always made grilled cheese when I stayed with her. I never thought anyone could top hers, but you just might have!"

"That's it!" Madison said, hitting her head as she talked. "Remember my Norwegian grandmother?"

The other three girls looked at Madison as if she had lost her mind.

"What on earth are you talking about, Madison?" Callie said.

"My grandmother was into family history. She searched our ancestors all the way back to a village in Norway—" Madison started explaining, but Callie interrupted.

"So, what does that have to do with Tom?"

"No listen," Madison continued. "She found information on her own grandmother in census records. It's easy to search census records online. Believe you me, if my grandmother can search census records online, I know

Aimee can. We can look up the census records for each of these soldiers. The government does a census every ten years. It's required."

"But even if we find an entry for each of these people in 1860, how is that going to help us? Tom was not yet married to Mattie, and they both died before the 1870 census. Any entry for a Tom will offer no further provable data. We're still at the same place. We won't know if it's our Tom."

Aimee hated to dismiss the suggestion, but it just was not quite right.

The girls looked to Callie. They knew she was the analytical, logical thinker of the group.

"Let me think for a moment," Callie said.

The girls remained quiet. They could almost see the wheels turning in Callie's head. It didn't take long for her face to change. They watched as Callie's eyes lit up, almost as if a light bulb just went off.

"I've got it!" Callie said, jumping up from her chair. "We don't look for Tom; we look in the 1870 North Carolina Census for a John and Sadie with one of these last names and an Andrew and Peter living with them. There is no reason to think that they were not still alive in 1870. It's a long shot, but worth the try."

"That's brilliant!" Aimee said.

"We have two computers. Aimee and Madison both have laptops. Let's work as two teams. Each team will only have eight names to search. I'll work with Megan, and Aimee and Mad can work together," Callie said. You two, take the first half of the list and we'll start with Thomas Russell."

The girls located a site on the internet that allowed users to search census records, so they got right to work.

Madison moaned with disappointment on their second try. She and Aimee had a positive hit on John Christianson in the 1870 North Carolina census, but when they examined the complete record, his wife's name was Charlotte, and the only child listed was a girl named Catherine. It was the closest that she and Aimee came with their entries.

Callie and Megan were not having any better results on their first three tries, and Callie was feeling that it was a lost cause. There were only two names left.

Callie entered her next possibility. She typed John Fraser to correspond with the next to the last Tom on the list. There was a John Fraser listed in the North Carolina 1870 census rolls. She opened up the complete census record. It was there for anyone to see. John and Sadie Fraser lived in Davie County, North Carolina in 1870. They had three children living with them: Andrew (age ten), Peter (age seven), and Molly (age five).

Callie was speechless for a moment. She sat back from the computer, took a deep breath, and announced, "Our Tom is Corporal Thomas Fraser of the Fourth North Carolina Regiment!"

The spirit heard Callie's pronouncement. It had been so long since he had heard his full name. He had almost forgotten how it sounded.

Thirty-seven

The next afternoon Callie sat in the parlor. Her three friends were on a shopping expedition, but Callie chose not to go with them. She needed to be alone. Tom's story had taken her back to the days right after the plane crash. She remembered the intensity of that time. She and her mother worked through their initial pain by jointly planning a memorial service for her father and Grandpa Matt. They invited their friends to join them to honor the two Monroe men. Callie remembered someone saying that the service was an opportunity for Lee Anne and Callie to say goodbye. At the service, Callie had the feeling that her father and Grandpa Matt were there with them. Did her father and grandfather also need to say goodbye? Perhaps a memorial service is not just for the living but also for those who died. Is that why Tom could not move to his next stage? He never had his own memorial service, his own chance to say goodbye.

Callie's moment of reflection was disturbed by the sound of the front door opening.

"We're back," Madison called out.

"I'm glad you're here.," Callie said, grateful that her good friends had returned. "I know what we have to do," she continued. "We need to hold a memorial service for Tom."

The girls looked at her, not understanding.

Callie told them of the memorial service for her father and grandfather, and they agreed with her—Tom deserved such a service.

The girls busied themselves for the next several days planning the details of Tom's memorial service carefully. They sent special invitations to Callie's mother, Bob McPherson, Jackie and Mark Hamilton, and they invited Mrs. Hodges as well.

The parlor was decorated with large bouquets of white and red roses, and the table beside the mantel held the historic artifacts representing Tom's life.

On Saturday afternoon, June 29, 2013, the guests arrived for the service and settled into the special chairs reserved for them in the parlor. The girls sat in the four additional chairs at the front of the room, with Callie sitting in the center chair, Madison on her left side, and Aimee and Megan on her right. The girls had been wearing shorts all summer but in honor of the solemn occasion, they each now wore a pretty summer dress.

Callie stood to address the group. There was utter silence in the room.

"We are here today to honor the life of Thomas Fraser. He has been part of the Calafont house since 1863, but he has only been known by the name Tom. This summer, my friends and I discovered Tom's story. We now know of his life before his spirit found a home in this limestone house. Our Tom was once Corporal Thomas Fraser of the 4th North Carolina Regiment. His name is listed among the soldiers of this regiment, part of Lee's Army of Northern Virginia. He marched with the regiment as they invaded the Cumberland Valley in the summer of 1863. My friend Madison will now speak of Tom's war service."

Madison rose and continued the story.

"Tom's regiment was involved in most of the major campaigns in the East. Apparently, he was a good soldier, for at some point, he was promoted to corporal.

"At the Battle of Seven Pines in June 1862, the 4th North Carolina Regiment earned the nickname *the Bloody Fourth*, due to the high level of casualties the regiment took in that battle. The bloody fighting did not end there for these men. The next September, they were at Antietam, stationed at the sunken road, now forever remembered as Bloody Lane. He survived Antietam, but the fighting was not yet over for Tom Fraser. His regiment saw action again at Fredericksburg and Chancellorsville. The next summer, Tom marched north again over South Mountain as part of Ewell's Corps. Their mission was to take the Pennsylvania state capital."

Mark Hamilton, the Civil War buff, listened closely as Madison talked. He had read first-person accounts of the fighting and glanced at gruesome pictures of dead bodies. He had visited the places that Madison mentioned. He had walked the lines of both Union and Confederate troops and stood at the Bloody Lane at Antietam and looked down from Marye's Heights at Fredericksburg. His involvement with the war previously had been academic. Now, he had a connection to these battles. The spirit that he saw when he was thirteen had actually lived through them.

Megan continued, "Throughout these long marches, Tom Fraser carried a knapsack containing his most precious possessions, which included his wedding picture. In it, he appears in his Confederate dress uniform, standing behind his wife, Mattie. This daguerreotype was on the piano among the Calafont family photos. In the attic, Madison and Callie found his knapsack. Inside were his Bible and two letters written to him in the spring of 1863. The first letter was from his loving wife. She shared with her husband that their love had created a baby that she now carried. She planned to name him Peter, after Tom's father, if it was a boy. Peter never had a chance to know either of his parents, as Mattie died bringing him into the world, and we now believe that Peter's father, Tom, died on Calafont land since we found the knapsack in the attic of this house. Many other members of the 4th North Carolina Regiment died at the Battle of Gettysburg a few days later."

Megan turned to Aimee, who picked up Tom's Bible.

In a voice that had a hint of her mother's British accent, Aimee said, "Tom obviously read this Bible frequently. Some pages are turned down, showing he often returned to a passage. They offered him comfort. He read one psalm in particular over and over again:

The Lord is my shepherd; I shall not want.
He maketh me like down in green pastures;
He leadeth me beside the still waters.
He restoreth my soul:
He leadeth me in the paths of righteousness for his name's sake:
Yea, though I walk through the valley of the shadow of death,
I will fear no evil.
Thou anointest my head with oil;
Surely goodness and mercy shall follow me all the days of my life;
And I will dwell in the house of the Lord forever.

Callie picked up where Madison left off.

"This psalm also comforted the mourners at Mattie's memorial service. Tom read of his wife's service in a letter from his loving brother, John, and his sister-in-law, Sadie. It is the second letter Tom carried in his knapsack. John and Sadie took Peter home with them and raised Tom's son in their home in Davie County, North Carolina We found an entry in the 1870 census for the family. Peter is listed as a member of John and Sadie's family."

The room was quiet as the guests absorbed what they were hearing.

Callie continued, "Megan has prepared a special gift for Mattie and Tom."

Megan moved to the piano and turned to the audience. "Tom was clearly Scottish by heritage, so I am going to sing an old ballad that he probably knew. It's about a man who will never meet his true love again in this mortal world."

She placed her hands on the keyboard and began to sing a soft and moving rendition of *The Bonnie Banks o' Loch Lomond.*

> *For ye'll take the high road*
> *And I'll take the low road*
> *And I'll be in Scotland afore ye*
> *For me and my true love will never meet again*
> *On the bonny bonny banks of Loch Lomond.*

Tom was listening to Megan sing. When she finished the chorus for the final time, he had tears in his eyes. He could hear Mattie, his own true love, singing this song in her kitchen.

Callie picked up the thread of the service when Megan finished playing the song.

"Tom also marked a passage in the New Testament. It is Christ's prayer to his father in heaven. We closed my own father's memorial service with this prayer. Please feel free to join me as I pray."

Callie began to recite the Lord's Prayer.

After a moment of silence at the prayer's end, Lee Anne stood up and hugged her daughter.

No one in the room knew that exactly a hundred fifty years ago to this very day, Sarah Calafont and her son, Matthew, buried the physical remains of an enemy soldier outside the house. On that day, so long ago, the mother and son prayed these same words over Tom's body. His remains were still under the Calafont rosebushes.

Thirty-eight

Tom felt moisture on his face from his tears as the memorial service drew to a close. Callie, so special, so like Amelia, had given him a great gift. He could feel the pull from outside the limestone house. He was almost ready to go, but there was one more thing that he needed to do. This time, he was going to say goodbye. He waited for the right moment.

Madison, Aimee, and Megan left right after the service. Their adventure was over. Each girl wanted to be in her own home for the upcoming Fourth of July holiday.

Callie watched their cars drive down the Calafont driveway and turn onto Walnut Bottom Road. She went back inside the limestone house and directly to the war room to dismantle the boards. Tom's board was complete. The holes in Amelia's board did not seem to matter right now. Callie was also ready for the summer to end.

Bob and the Hamiltons had also returned to their own busy lives. Just Lee Anne and Callie remained in the house. They planned to leave for D.C. in the morning, right after breakfast.

After her mom retired early to her bedroom with a novel, Callie roamed around downstairs. She went into the library where, a lifetime ago, Mark Hamilton had read a will that changed her life. Then she walked into the parlor. She sat on Amelia's piano bench and absently played a few notes on the keyboard.

For the last time, the curtains flared out. Callie felt the chill in the room and looked up from the keyboard. There, in front of her, was Tom. It was as if he had stepped out of his wedding picture; however, the black and white photo did not do him justice. It took color to bring out the blond streaks from the sun in his light brown hair and the deep blue of his eyes.

"I expected that you'd be here tonight," Callie said, realizing that she was not a bit surprised to see Tom in front of her. "You are leaving, aren't you, Tom?"

The apparition nodded his head yes.

"I'm glad that you came to say goodbye. I know Mattie is waiting for you."

Tom Fraser's smile lit up his face. It went all the way to his eyes.

"Can you do me one favor?" Callie asked.

Tom affirmatively shook his head.

"Please tell Amelia 'thank you' for me when you see her."

Tom raised his hand to his forehead and saluted Callie. He then disappeared.

"Rest in peace, Tom Fraser," Callie said.

Part

IV

Thirty-nine

Washington, D.C.

Six Years Later

It was a little after four in the afternoon when Callie unlocked the door of a brick house on a quiet street in northwest Washington, D.C.

"Anyone home?" she shouted.

Lee Anne appeared and quickly pulled her daughter into a warm embrace. "Callie, you're here early. I wasn't expecting you for another hour. How was the wedding?" she asked.

"It was lovely. We were outside and the weather co-operated. A perfect fall day. We all stood on an over-look in the Blue Ridge Mountains; down below was the Shenandoah River. There were only about thirty guests, including the wedding party," Callie said.

"You know I'm partial to small weddings," Lee Anne said.

Callie knew her mother was thinking of her own wedding. Lee Anne and Bob were married in the parlor of the Calafont house almost six years ago at Christmastime. Callie was her mother's maid of honor, and Jackie and Mark Hamilton were the witnesses. Mrs. Hodges insisted on baking and decorating the wedding cake herself.

"I always thought that of the four of you, Megan would be the first one to marry. One never can really predict the future," Lee Anne said as she thought about the four girls who remained close friends.

"I agree. I always thought that Megan would walk down the aisle first. I was just as surprised as you when Madison called me two months ago and said she was getting married. The wedding came together quickly. She wanted to be married before her basketball season started. Her girl's high school team went to the state playoffs last year. You know Madison when it comes to one of her goals. She intends to be the first coach to bring a state championship trophy home to the high school. She's not going to let a wedding get in her way. Madison and Doug seem perfect for each other. It's a good thing that as a sportscaster he understands her priorities."

Lee Ann smiled at her daughter's description of Madison. The nickname Mad still applied. She had really not changed that much since their days at Ada Lovelace.

"Speaking of Megan," Callie said, "she loves her job at The Kennedy Center. She describes herself as a very lowly production assistant, but she's learning a lot about staging plays and dealing with the inevitable crisis that always seems to happen right before the curtain is supposed to rise. She says that it's all preparing her for her future. She wants someday to be a director at a community playhouse. No man in sight, as far as I can tell, but it doesn't seem to bother her in the least."

All of a sudden, a blonde-headed ball of energy ran toward Callie.

"Callie, you're here! I have been waiting for you all day!"

"All day?" Callie said, smiling. "I find that hard to believe."

Callie teased the little girl and kissed the top her head.

"Have you given your mother any new ideas for her next book?"

Lee Anne's books were gaining in popularity. The little blonde girl in her stories always managed to get into trouble. The illustrations looked very much like the youngster who was now squirming as her older sister tickled her.

"I may just have come up with a new title by watching the two of you," Lee Anne said. "How about *Amelia and the Tickle Monster*? I think it might be a good addition to *Amelia and the Lost Kitten* and *Amelia Plants a Garden*. My publisher is eager for another title in the series."

"What do you think of that idea?" Callie said to her sister.

Amelia Anne McPherson just giggled.

"Amelia, you need to pick up your toys before your

father gets home. Callie and I want to catch up," Lee Anne said in her firmest mother's voice.

Amelia ran back to her playroom; she never walked if she could run.

"She has so much energy," Lee Anne said. "She wears me out. I don't remember feeling that way when you were her age, but I was twenty-three then. I'll be forty-three on my next birthday, and sometimes I feel my age."

"Well, you look pretty good for someone over forty, but more importantly, you seem content," Callie said, looking at her mother.

"Thanks, I am. Bob just called and said he'd be home around six. I have lasagna in the oven. I'll turn it on low and we can sit and talk. Do you want a glass of wine?" Lee Anne asked her daughter.

"Sounds good," Callie said.

Callie tried to push back her mood. She looked around the den. She liked this house. Her mother and Bob bought it right after they learned that they were expecting. Callie knew she was always welcome here, but it would never really be her home.

Is this the problem? Callie thought. *Am I just feeling that I do not have roots?*

All weekend, she was bothered by her increasing feeling of restlessness. She needed to understand a situation in order to deal with it. Madison always told her she overanalyzed everything and maybe she was just thinking too much. She should be happy. Everyone thought she had a perfect situation. Right after graduation from Harvard Business School, she landed a coveted position at a Wall Street investment firm. She had the chance to meet business leaders who made financial decisions that affected the world economy.

It looked like she had it all: mentors who listened to her and guided her, senior management pleased with her performance, and a circle of acquaintances—even if she could not actually call them friends—who were available if she needed company. She was living the life that someone with her credentials was supposed to be living. She even looked the part, with a closet full of the right clothes and shoes.

It was not just Madison's wedding. Her feelings had been building for a while, long before Madison asked her to be her maid of honor. It was not that she was feeling desperate to be in a relationship. At twenty-three, she knew that she had plenty of time for marriage and children. All her friends had found their way. She was the only one who seemingly was lost.

Lee Anne handed her daughter a glass of Chardonnay and they settled into comfortable chairs in the den. Lee Anne was a little worried. Her mother's instinct told her that something was bothering her oldest daughter.

"How's New York?" Lee Anne asked.

Callie played with her wine glass and took a moment to think about how to answer her mother's question.

"Boring," she finally said.

In saying the word, Callie knew she had identified part of the problem. She was bored with the endless focus on money and deals. She enjoyed predicting which stocks would increase in worth, and she was very good at analyzing market trends; it was fun, it was like solving puzzles. But she wanted more from life. She just didn't know what *more* meant.

Lee Anne raised an eyebrow and waited for her daughter to elaborate. People usually did not use that word to describe the financial capital of the world.

"Mom, I think I am going to resign from my job right after Christmas. I want to take some time to think about things, and I cannot do it in the intensity of Wall Street."

"If that is what you want to do, you should do it. Do you want to go to Brussels to see Aimee?" Lee Anne said.

There it was again. Aimee had also found herself. For the last two years, she had been a cyber security expert for NATO.

"No, I will want to go see her at some point, but not now. I need to figure some things out first."

An idea hit Callie as she talked to her mother.

"I think I would like to spend some time at the Calafont house. Maybe I can relax there and come up with what I want to do with my life."

"Well, I know Mrs. Hodges will be glad to have you," Lee Anne said.

Forty

The Limestone House

January 2019

There are approximately two hundred miles separating New York City from the Cumberland Valley. For Callie, the distance could not really be measured in miles.

Callie left Midtown Manhattan early on a cold January morning. She was closing a chapter of her life and felt a little sad. She had sublet her New York apartment and left her furniture for the next occupant. Her car was loaded with the outward symbols of her New York life. She had a small overnight bag with her immediate necessities on the seat beside her. Her business suits and silk blouses were on hangers in the backseat. On the floor of the backseat were two heavy boxes full of personal items and books. Three suitcases containing the rest of her clothes and a box of shoes were in her trunk.

She drove through the Holland Tunnel and headed south. Callie's mood began to lift by the time she reached

Newark. She only stopped her car once in New Jersey to get a sandwich, fill her car with gas, and to buy a Diet Coke and a large bag of M&Ms. The skies were clear all the way to the Pennsylvania line. On the other side of Allentown, it began to spit snow. As she crossed the Susquehanna at Harrisburg, the snow began to pick up, and by the time she turned onto Walnut Bottom Road, there were already two inches on the ground.

Callie could see the limestone house from the beginning of the driveway. She felt a warm sense of peace. It was a pretty sight, almost as if she was looking at a Christmas card. Only a horse-drawn sleigh was needed to complete the nostalgic picture.

She was tired after the long drive, and it was good to turn off the car. The cold snowy air hit her when she opened the car door. She grabbed the overnight bag and ran to the house.

The lights were on in the downstairs rooms. Callie felt the house was welcoming her home. She rang the bell on the front door. She knew that it was officially her house, but she was conscious that it was also Mrs. Hodges' home. It was only a minute before the older woman opened the door. Mamie Hodges had not aged much in six years. There were a few more gray hairs and perhaps an additional inch around her waist, but her kind face and big smile were the same.

"I was getting worried about you," Mrs. Hodges said. "The weatherman is predicting at least eight inches. I am so glad that you got here before the roads got really bad. Come on in and warm up. I know you will want something warm to drink. I'll make you a cup of hot chocolate."

Callie smiled and hugged the woman who was like a grandmother to her.

"Bless you, Mrs. Hodges. You always know what I need. Give me chocolate and I'm content."

"Now, you get out of that coat and come into the kitchen," Mrs. Hodges said. "Keep me company while I fill your mug. I made brownies this afternoon, and there's a hot pot of soup on the stove just waiting for you."

Mrs. Hodges' kitchen was one of Callie's favorite places. The two talked for several hours. Callie heard all about Mrs. Hodges' own daughter and family, who lived in Florida, and Callie entertained her with the latest adventures of young Amelia.

Callie was relieved that Mrs. Hodges didn't ask any questions about how long she intended to stay or why she decided to leave New York. She did not want to explain that she had no definite plans.

Mrs. Hodges noticed Callie's eyes beginning to look heavy, and she realized that it was time to call it a night.

"I have your room all ready for you," Mrs. Hodges said. "Now, you just crawl into bed and go to sleep. Don't worry about getting up early in the morning. Sleep as late as you'd like. I may not be here when you get up. I have to set up for a church luncheon. Hopefully, the roads will be passable."

Callie touched the bannister as she walked up the stairs. She could tell that Mrs. Hodges had recently polished the wood. She loved its smooth feel. Mrs. Hodges called the room at the top of the stairs *her* room, but to Callie it would always be "Aunt Amelia's room." It looked just the same as it did six years ago, when Callie found her aunt's last note. She crawled into the large comfortable bed and snuggled under the homemade quilt. It felt so cozy. It did not take long for her to fall asleep.

Callie slept late the next morning. When she awoke, she got out of bed and looked out the window. Sometime during the night, the snow had stopped. Callie guessed that the weather predications regarding the snowfall had been a little low. There were at least ten inches of powdery snow on the ground. Mr. Quinn had already plowed the driveway, and Callie could see the tracks of Mrs. Hodges' car in the snow. The sun was shining, but it looked very cold outside.

It was nice to have the house all to herself. Mrs. Hodges left her a note. As instructed, Callie helped herself to the fresh scones and heaped some of Mrs. Hodges' preserves on them. She walked around the house. The sunroom windows let in the bright morning sun. Callie would always think of it as the war room. She smiled, remembering Madison's careful calligraphy and their detailed sticky notes. She looked out the big window. She could not see the rose bushes under all the snow. She next went

through the dining room and into the library. There was not a speck of dust on any of the furniture. She finally settled into a comfortable chair next to the piano in the parlor. The room looked the same as it had at the beginning of June six years ago, but Callie knew that without Tom's spirit, it was different. She tried to define the difference but could only come up with the words *warm and peaceful* to now describe the parlor.

Callie knew that she should unpack her car; however, that would take energy, so she just put it off. She heard Mrs. Hodges return safely home, but still she did not leave her comfortable place. She felt no pressure to do anything. For the first time in many months, Callie relaxed, and in doing so, the tension she had been carrying left her.

The next day, Mr. Quinn brought a load of wood into the house and Callie made a fire in the parlor's large fireplace. She curled up in front of its warmth with a book from the library. It was so pleasant that she followed the same pattern for the next several nights. During the afternoons, she played a few easy pieces on the piano. She would never have Megan's skills, but the piano had such a wonderful tone that even her attempts at music sounded good.

One morning, bundled in a wool coat and boots, Callie wandered aimlessly outside. By the stream marking the edge of Calafont land, she saw some wild animal tracks in the snow. She thought they were probably deer, but she didn't really know. She thought that her Calafont ancestors would have known which animals drank from their stream.

Callie ended up at the old barn, where Mr. Quinn was working on the snow plow, apparently expecting to use it again soon. She listened as he told her that the wooly bear caterpillars were especially fat this fall and that they were in for a hard winter. She smiled. She had no doubt that he would also be able to recognize the animal tracks.

Callie returned to the house that belonged on this land. She felt very close to those who had previously lived there.

It was five days before Callie got around to moving her clothes and suitcases from her car into Amelia's room. By then, most of the snow had melted. She hung up her business suits and blouses in the closet. She had no intention of wearing them anytime soon, but there was no reason for them to become wrinkled. She arranged her shoes on the floor of the closet. Amelia's comb and brush were still on the antique chest of drawers. Callie put her own brush next to Amelia's and opened the suitcase containing her underwear and sweaters. She pulled the brass handles and opened the first of the five drawers of the old dresser. She placed her lingerie in it and her socks and nightgowns in the second drawer. Her woolen sweaters came next. She had brought five with her, and they took up much of the third drawer. The sweaters went perfectly with her jeans and other pants, which she placed in the fourth drawer. She still had some odds and ends left, so she opened the bottom drawer.

"That's strange," Callie said aloud.

This drawer was not as deep as the other four drawers. She stood back and looked at the delicate chest, poised on its curved legs. From the outside, it looked as if all five drawers should be the same size, but that was not the case. The bottom drawer was shallower. She knelt on the floor to see inside it. The wood was smooth to her touch and there was no obvious difference between it and the other drawers. She felt the bottom. There was nothing that indicated why it was not as deep as the others. Callie ran her hand around the side. She felt a small bump and pressed it.

For the first time in seventy-three years, a compartment opened. Inside, Amelia's memories were just as she had left them in August of 1946.

Forty-one

Callie carefully lifted the photos, letters, and the leather-bound book out of the secret compartment. She turned on a light to get a better look at the material and sat on the floor. She examined the photos first.

Several photos were of young women dressed in clothes from the 1940s. They appeared to be about her own age. On the back of each photo, the woman's name was written in handwriting that Callie recognized

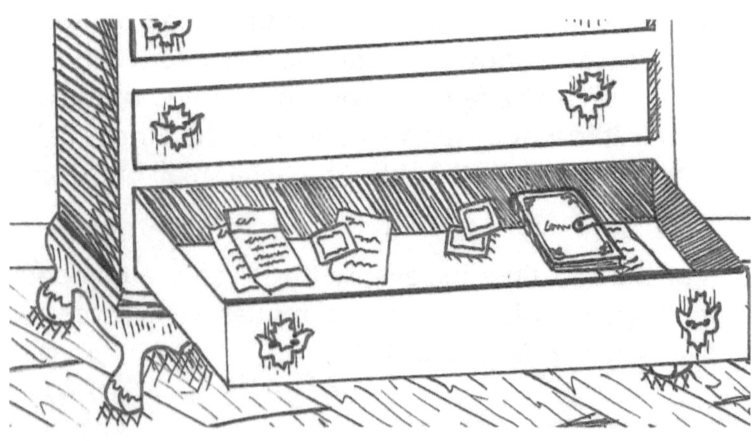

as Amelia's. One photo showed all the women gathered around a table. In the middle of the table was a birthday cake with the words 'Happy Birthday, Amelia' written on it. In the center of the picture, Amelia Calafont's lips were poised to blow out the candles on the cake. Several of the other girls were clapping. Callie thought of Madison, Aimee, and Megan, as they held a party just like this one for her last birthday.

The next picture was different. It was of a stately building. Callie turned it over and saw that Amelia had written Arlington Hall, 1945 on the back. Callie picked up her phone and did a search for the building's name, immediately finding the information that she was seeking:

Arlington Hall was the home of the United States Army's cryptographic work during World War II. It was the American version of Britain's Bletchley Park. Partly because men were involved in military operations, the Army turned to bright young women, many recent graduates of the elite women colleges known as the 'Seven Sisters.' These women proved very good at code breaking, and their efforts had a significant effect on shortening the war.

"So, that's it—another mystery solved!" Callie said aloud.

It was clear. Amelia Calafont was a code breaker during World War II.

Callie continued searching and found more articles that described these women and their contributions to America. The profile of a code breaker as a bright young woman, often a teacher with extraordinary math abilities, fit Amelia Calafont to a tee. Apparently, Amelia was very good at her job.

An envelope was paperclipped to the picture. Inside was an official commendation praising Amelia's contribution to the war effort. The accompanying letter contained a strict warning that she must never talk about her work. It was still classified.

Callie picked up the next photo in the stack. It was of a young man dressed in a World War II army uniform. She could tell by his insignia that he was a major. Callie turned it over. Amelia had written his name there: Michael. *So, this was Michael,* Callie thought. The love of Amelia's life. She could see it. Not movie star handsome, but he was good looking. It was a formal picture, so he was not really smiling, but he had very nice eyes.

There was an envelope underneath the photo that contained two handwritten pages. The first was from a colonel. Movingly, he wrote:

I feel I know you, Amelia.

Michael talked of your beautiful red hair so often. He asked me to make sure that you receive this letter if anything happened to him. It grieves me that I must deliver it to you.

I sent Michael on his last assignment. It was one of those necessary decisions that war forces commanders to make. Michael saved many men that night, although he lost his own life. I have put him in for the Distinguished Service Cross. I have had no man in my command who deserved it more.

The attached letter was from Michael.

My darling, if you are reading this letter, our dreams will not have a chance to be.

Callie felt the tears on her cheek as she read Michael's goodbye note that was only meant for Amelia's eyes.

She had been sitting on the floor for a long time and stood up to stretch her legs. She looked out the window and was surprised to see that the sun had already set. She had been in Amelia's room the whole afternoon. Only the leather-bound book remained for Callie to examine. She opened it and again saw Amelia's handwriting. The book was full of handwritten pages.

Callie realized that she had not eaten since breakfast, so she took the book downstairs with her. Mrs. Hodges had gone out to visit a friend. Callie fixed a salad for herself and ate it quickly. She took the book and a cup of hot tea into the parlor, where she sat in front of the warm fire. Callie opened the book. It was Amelia's diary of her life in Washington, D.C. during World War II.

The journal started with Amelia leaving the Cumberland Valley on a train bound for the nation's capital. She was twenty-four, just a year older than Callie.

Today, right before my train pulled out of the station, Emily handed me this journal and told me to record my experiences. I do not know what to expect. I have been recruited to work for the war effort. I have no idea what that means, but soon I will find out.

With these words, Amelia Calafont began her journey of playing a role in defeating the Axis powers, the monumental struggle of the twentieth century and of her generation.

Amelia did not write every day. As Callie learned, Amelia was often too busy to write about her day. Passages were full of the fun times she shared with the girls who lived with her at Arlington Farms. The nation's capital was full of Government Girls, as they were called. Some actually worked with her. Others were secretaries in one of the structures that cropped up almost overnight as the city mobilized for war. She told of the soldiers who temporarily were part of their lives. They came through Washington on their way to someplace else, many headed to join the fighting in Europe. The girls entertained them at USO dances and the men took them to dinner. Many of the men were looking for someone to remember them when they left. The G.I.s gave the girls their addresses, hoping to receive letters, and the G.I.s sent letters back to them. Some of her friends were writing letters to as many as twenty soldiers. Amelia never wrote in her journal about her actual work. It was a secret that she could never share.

Callie read quickly, fascinated with her great aunt's story. Some passages had special meaning for her, as they involved names she recognized. In one such passage, Amelia worried that she had hurt Bill Hamilton, Mark Hamilton's father. Apparently, he was in love with her, but Amelia did not return his feelings—she turned down his marriage proposal.

Another passage caught Callie's eyes. Amelia wrote of her grandfather's funeral and Emily's announcement that she was in love with Stephen Monroe, Callie's great-grandfather. She also wrote of the night she met a young major at Arlington Farms. Callie smiled at Amelia's description of their romance. It sounded so sweet and innocent when she wrote of the feel of Michael's hand in hers.

It was late when Callie finished reading the diary. Her aunt's story appeared to end abruptly, so Callie thought that Amelia had finished writing, but when she turned over three blank pages, another passage appeared:

August 1946,

I have come home to the limestone house. The war is over. Michael is gone. I have cried. Now I can dry my tears.

I have received a gift. My father and I are developing a special relationship. Each morning we discuss business issues. Together, we look at the stock market reports. I have taken to analyzing market trends. It reminds me of the work I did during the war. It is fun, like the puzzles that I used to solve with Grandfather. It has taken me away from my pain.

My father and I were never really close before. Emily and I had Tom as our special friend when we were young. Grandfather read to us, held us on his knee, and told us family stories. Father was always busy with his work. Now, Father and I have a shared interest. It is a special bond we will always have.

Father paid me the ultimate compliment today. He offered me a position at his bank. He told me that I would be the first woman to hold such a position in the county. He could see me as the president of Cumberland Mutual Trust someday, or I could hold another important position. He did not say this because I am his daughter. Father would never react emotionally when it comes to business. He made the offer because he admires my financial aptitude. It is a great honor. I am flattered and tempted, but this is not where my spirit is leading me.

Tom has taught me that our spirit is far more important than our physical body. My spirit is leading me to make a difference. I know my work in a small way made a difference during the war. I do not have an aversion to working with money and growing it through investments. In fact, I enjoy it. I find it fun. However, if I was doing it to make a living, it would be a different story. I would grow bored with it. My spirit calls me in a different direction. I am to teach children. Michael and I will never have the children that were part of our dreams, but there are children who need my love. Here, I can make a difference.

I will have a good life living in this limestone house. It is where I was born. It is where I am to stay. My spirit will be content here. I am no longer sad when I think of Michael. I remember the small

Callie was still after she closed Amelia's journal. She had always assumed that Amelia never had a chance to use her gifts because she was a woman. She thought that Amelia was relegated to teaching because that was one of the few jobs available to her. Obviously, this was not the case. Amelia Calafont had the chance to be a trailblazer, to be a role model for women. She rejected that life. Callie understood her aunt's use of the word boring. She herself used that word to describe her own life to her mother. Callie's spirit was also calling her to make a difference, not in teaching, as Amelia's spirit called, but in some meaningful way that was not yet clear.

In the fireplace, the embers were dying down and Callie felt a chill. Her bed with its warm covers called to her. Tomorrow morning would be here soon. It would bring another day to think and ponder.

When Callie awoke the next morning, she no longer felt lethargic. She jumped out of bed quickly. Sometime during the night, she came up with a plan. It was short on details, but she knew her way forward. It was time to leave the limestone house. She was going back to Washington. Amelia Calafont had found meaning there when she was her age. Although she didn't see herself working for the government, Callie knew she had gifts and skills to offer; it was only a matter of finding the right situation in which to use them. Callie had faith that a door would soon open, and when it did, she would walk through it. She had contacts in D.C. She would be with friends and family. Most importantly, it gave her a chance to be part of her younger sister's life.

The next day, as Callie prepared to leave the limestone house and before saying goodbye to Mrs. Hodges, she returned her aunt's memories to the secret compartment. Someday, she knew she would bring Amelia McPherson to the old limestone house and would share with her younger sister the story of the summer when four high school girls brought peace to Tom's spirit. And then she would show her the antique dresser with the secret compartment and tell Amelia Calafont's namesake about the incredible woman who changed their lives.

Forty-two

Washington, D.C.

Spring 2019

Jackie Hamilton was the chair of the Gala for the Children, a major charity event benefiting the local children's hospital in Washington, D.C. This year, Tristan Industries was the gala's major sponsor.

James Tristan's story was classic Americana. His father died when he was very young, and he was raised by a hard-working single mother. Jim was working his way through college when a benefactor saw promise in the young man and gave him a break. Jim made the most of the opportunity and he now had more money than he could count. At seventy-two, he was ready to disengage from the business world. His oldest son had taken over the reins of Tristan Industries and was running it well. James Tristan wanted to "pay it forward," and he had a plan. He wanted to find deserving people who just needed a break, and he would give it to them.

Jim Tristan never did anything casually. His efforts were always well-planned and structured. He created a nonprofit foundation to carry out his vision. He knew there was not just one formula that would work for all deserving candidates. He intended to tailor his efforts to the specific needs of each one. Some would receive scholarships, and others would be loaned seed money for an entrepreneurial venture. If a candidate's small business was floundering, Jim would offer them temporary managerial guidance. He needed some bright young person to help him implement his ideas. He had interviewed a handful of candidates but, so far, none were exactly right. He had a picture in his mind of a smart, creative person with imagination, who had leadership and excellent business skills, someone who could take charge of a project and run with it. Most of all, he needed someone who embraced his vision. Jackie Hamilton had told him that Callie Monroe was just the person he needed, and after meeting Callie, he knew Jackie was right.

The Tristan Foundation was exactly the place for Callie to use her gifts. Their offices were located in a small restored nineteenth century rowhouse on Capitol Hill. As luck would have it, Megan's roommate moved to Los Angeles right after Thanksgiving. Her apartment was the perfect location for Callie, just a few blocks from the foundation. In less than a month after leaving the Calafont house, Callie's life had fallen into place.

The second week of March 2019 found Callie in a particularly good mood, as she had identified a candidate for the foundation. The young couple's small computer graphics business was ready to expand when the wife was hurt in a nasty car accident. The money that they had saved for the expansion went out the door to pay for her care. Not only would their dreams have to be put on hold, but the business was in danger of not meeting its obligations. Banks had rejected their loan requests, and they were at risk for losing it all if they didn't catch a break. They were just the type of people the foundation was established to help. Not only was Jim Tristan paying back his own benefactor, but Callie believed that she was paying back Amelia Calafont.

Callie wanted to celebrate, and chocolate would fit the bill. She walked to her favorite coffee shop and ordered a large caramel latte. After carefully scrutinizing the pastries, she added a chocolate éclair to her order. Balancing the hot liquid in one hand and her treat in the other, she turned around and collided with a man carrying a cup of hot coffee. Hot liquid drenched her business suit, and she dropped her éclair, chocolate side down, onto the floor.

"Oh no, not my eclair!" Callie exclaimed.

The man tried to hide his smile when he looked at the attractive auburn-haired woman who was staring at the ruined pastry. He was amused that she didn't seem to notice the liquid from her skirt dripping onto her stylish high heels. Most of the professional young women he knew would be more concerned about their appearance and not a pastry that easily could be replaced.

"I can't do much about your clothes, but I can get you another éclair," he said.

It didn't take long for the man to return with a new cup of coffee for himself, as well as a replacement for Callie's order. He handed the latte and pastry to her and said, "We should probably sit down and drink these before we spill them again"

The man had a nice smile and no wedding ring, so Callie agreed to join him. For a moment, Callie thought that she had met him before, but quickly dismissed the idea. The men around Capitol Hill all tended to look a little alike to her.

"Since my coffee already met your latte, I guess I should introduce myself. I'm Adam Carter."

Callie laughed and said, "Callie Monroe," before biting into her éclair. It tasted just as good as it looked.

"Do you work on the Hill?" Adam asked.

"Yes, but not in the way you mean," Callie said. "I'm not a congressional staffer. I'm the program director at a small nonprofit, just around the corner."

"Which one?" Adam asked.

"The Tristan Foundation," Callie said.

"I've read about Jim Tristan. It sounds like he has a really unique idea about how to give back. I like the idea of passing on your blessings to others. Perhaps, one day I'll be in the position to do so."

"In the meantime, what do you do?" Callie asked.

"I'm a visiting fellow at Georgetown."

Callie looked at him with renewed interest. She was a little tired of the self-absorbed politicos that she was used to meeting on Capitol Hill.

"I'd love to hear more about your work with the foundation," Adam said, "but, unfortunately, I have a meeting in ten minutes. I hate being late, so I better run. Would you care to meet for drinks some night this week and tell me more about it? I'm busy tonight, but I have no plans yet for tomorrow night."

Callie thought Adam seemed nice enough, and she liked his eyes, so she thought it should be safe enough to meet him in a public space.

"I can do tomorrow," Callie said. "Where would you like to meet, and what time?"

Adam mentioned a popular bar and suggested they meet at five-thirty.

When Adam left, Callie looked down at her clothes. She had just enough time to run back to her apartment and change before her meeting with Mr. Tristan to discuss her proposed candidate.

The bar was crowded when Callie arrived Wednesday night. She found Adam saving a chair for her in the back area, close to the dartboard. When he smiled at her, Callie smiled back. She noticed again his nice smile and great eyes.

Callie sat down in the chair next to Adam and ordered a hard cider. They exchanged the usual *get to know you* biographies. Callie was surprised to learn that Adam was originally from Omaha, Nebraska, not all that far from Lawrence, Kansas.

Callie briefly shared her story of inheriting an old limestone house in the Cumberland Valley from an aunt she'd never met, and Adam talked about his family's land on the Nebraskan prairie. The conversation flowed easily.

By six thirty, the noise in the bar area was so loud that it made having a conversation almost impossible, so Adam suggested they go someplace to get something to eat.

Over dinner, Callie smiled when Adam apologized for being a meat eater, explaining that he knew it wasn't necessarily the cool thing to be these days, but he really wanted a cheeseburger. Callie put him at ease by telling him that she had been known to eat meat on occasion, too, and they both laughed.

A week after their first dinner out together, Callie invited Adam to go to the opening of a new play at the Kennedy Center. Megan had given her the two tickets, and she was eager to see Adam again, so this was the perfect opportunity to reconnect. In return, Adam took her out to dinner again, this time to a really nice restaurant. Soon, the pair was seeing each other two to three times a week.

Forty-three

I will always want to be in Washington, D.C., in the spring, Callie thought to herself.

She was sitting on the top step of the Lincoln Memorial, waiting for Adam to join her. It was a bright Saturday afternoon in late April. The cherry blossoms had already peaked, but new flowering trees were taking their place. Tulips and other flowers were everywhere she looked. She observed the people below her, a mixed bag. The tourists were easy to pick out, as many had guidebooks in their hands and were dragging children along for the "educational experience." She heard a mother behind her trying to explain Abraham Lincoln's greatness to a boy about ten. Her son looked bored.

Callie was more interested in the couples that walked along the wide sidewalk in front of her than the tourists. These days, she noticed couples in a way that she never had before. She hoped that they were all as happy as she was. She thought of Amelia and Michael. *I wonder if they walked in front of the memorial in the summer of 1944 holding hands?* she thought. She remembered Amelia's description of the feel of Michael's hand in hers. Callie now understood what she meant.

She saw Adam in the crowd. Callie wondered if he really stood out from all the others or was she just seeing an Adam that others did not see? She waved at him. He was right on time. It was one of the many things that she liked about him. She watched as he climbed the steps toward her.

Adam smiled and took Callie's hand to pull her to her feet.

Callie held Adam's hand as they watched the people below for a moment, and then they both turned to look at Lincoln.

The colossal figure carved in marble, with Lincoln's speeches etched on the memorial's wall, never failed to move Callie.

"I've always liked this statue," Adam said.

The couple walked over to the area where Lincoln's second inaugural address was etched and read his words. The last paragraph moved Callie:

With malice toward none; with charity for all; with firmness in the right, as God gives us to see the right, let us strive on to finish the work we are in; to bind up the nation's wounds; to care for him who shall have borne the battle, and for his widow, and his orphan—to do all which may achieve and cherish a just and lasting peace, among ourselves, and with all nations.

She thought the address was all the more powerful because Lincoln delivered it just six weeks before he was shot.

Together, Callie and Adam then moved to the plaque containing the words of the Gettysburg Address.

"What powerful speeches these are," Callie said.

Adam nodded in agreement and then said, "Did you ever visit Gettysburg? You said that your family's ancestral home is in the Cumberland Valley, right?"

"Yes, it's only about thirty miles from Gettysburg. Three of my friends and I spent a morning at the battlefield the summer I turned seventeen," Callie replied without elaborating further.

"The battlefield holds special significance for me," Adam said. "My great-great … I have to stop to figure how many greats to put in front of the word grandfather … died there. The family never knew where his body fell. He fought for the Confederacy and his body was never returned to the family."

Callie looked at him in surprise. "The Confederacy? I thought Nebraska was in the Union. You seem so midwestern to me, not at all Southern."

"I am midwestern. The Confederate soldier's son left the South in the 1880s," Adam said. Stopping briefly, Adam continued, "Let's walk around the Mall, and if you're interested, I'll tell you about him. I always liked his story."

"Of course, I'm interested. I'd love to hear about him," Callie said.

"He was only twenty when he went west. He really had no ties in the south. His immediate family was all gone. Not only did his father die at Gettysburg, but his mother died the day he was born. Even though he was raised by caring family members, there was nothing keeping him in North Carolina. He left the South behind and began his own family story out west.

"He staked out a homestead claim on the Nebraska prairie. He soon found that the land was not truly free. The price to own it was back-breaking work. Grasshoppers ate his initial wheat crop, and his first winter out west, he almost froze to death during a blizzard. There were some years with too little rain and other years with too much rain. Unlike many, he stuck it out and was rewarded with a free and clear title to his land. The land is still in my family. My uncle grows wheat on it."

All of a sudden, Callie felt strange. It was still warm, but she was chilled. She pushed the feeling away and focused her attention on Adam's story.

"You seem to know a lot about him?" she remarked.

"I was raised on stories about him," Adam said. "I spent a month with my mother's father every July when I was a kid. I never tired of hearing my grandfather's stories. He showed me where his grandfather's sod house once stood. Granddad taught me important lessons by using his own grandfather's life as an example. I can still hear him say, *Adam, remember, you have my Grandfather Peter's spirit in you. His blood runs in your veins.*'"

My grandfather has been gone for years, but I still miss him."

Callie again felt the strange chill. She understood how important a grandfather could be. She thought perhaps that was why she was finding Adam's story particularly meaningful.

In an effort to push away her uncomfortable sensations, Callie said, "I know what you mean. My Grandpa Matt was special to me."

"I didn't mean to get sentimental. Do you want to continue walking around the Mall?" Adam asked.

Callie nodded affirmatively and was relieved when the strange feeling went away. She was happy when Adam took her hand as they walked.

From the banks of the reflecting pool, they looked back at the memorial. The view almost took Callie's breath away. They continued walking, not really noticing the crowd of people enjoying the beautiful day.

Because the weather was so lovely, Callie and Adam decided not to visit any of the museums indoors; they would visit the museums some cold winter day.

Callie looked down at her hand in Adam's and again thought of Amelia. She understood now why her aunt remembered the feel of Michael's hand on hers.

The couple walked for hours before they grew tired and decided to stop for dinner. When Adam asked for the check, Callie watched him sign his name to the credit card receipt, Adam F. Carter. She liked watching his hands; he had long tapered fingers.

"What does the F stand for?" she asked.

"My mother's family name, Fraser."

She looked into his eyes. She now understood why she always felt that she had previously met Adam. She thought, *I've seen his eyes before. He has Tom's eyes.*

"Callie, you look like you are someplace else? Are you ok?" Adam asked.

Callie took a deep breath and said, "I just remembered an old family story. Someday, I'll tell it to you."

Adam smiled, a smile that lit up his deep blue eyes.

"I'll hold you to it," he said. "We have the rest of our lives to hear each other's stories. Are you ready to go?"

Callie nodded her head as Adam reached out and took her hand in his. As they walked out of the restaurant, Callie knew that she would find the right time to tell him that Peter Fraser's father did not die on the battlefield of Gettysburg; he died in the parlor of a limestone house in the Cumberland Valley.

Epilogue

Callie took Adam to the Calafont house the week after he proposed. In the parlor where Tom Fraser died, Callie Anne Monroe told Adam the story of the spirit of a Confederate soldier who once found a home here. She showed him Tom and Mattie's wedding picture. The resemblance between Thomas Fraser and Adam Fraser Carter was undeniable.

Adam held Tom's Bible in his hands. He smiled when he read Mattie's letter to her beloved husband, announcing that they were going to have a baby. He thought of his own grandfather who loved the man whom Tom and Mattie created. He openly cried when he read John and Sadie's letter telling Tom that Mattie was dead.

Callie told Adam of the summer when four teenage girls discovered Tom's identity, and she could tell he was moved by her account of the memorial service for Tom. She then told him of the night Tom's spirit said goodbye to her.

Adam pulled the woman he loved into his arms. He thanked her from the bottom of his heart for bringing peace to the spirit who once lived in the limestone house.

About the Book

Author's Notes

This is a work of fiction. The Calafont family and their home, Callie's family and friends, the Ada Lovelace Academy, and the law firm of Hamilton, Hamilton, and Blakely, only exist in the pages of this book.

The historic context of the story, however, is accurate. Homes built of limestone still dot the landscape of the Cumberland Valley of Pennsylvania. In June of 1863, the Fourth North Carolina regiment marched down the Walnut Bottom road from Shippensburg to Carlisle as part of Robert E. Lee's ill-fated plan to invade the North. Although there was no Tom Fraser in the regiment, it was formed by men from central and western North Carolina. The regiment fought in most of the major Civil War battles in the east. However, they were not at the First Battle of Manassas. I like this little detail. It means that Tom Fraser's character could not possibly have fired the musket that killed Sarah Calafont's husband John.

My house is full of books on the Gettysburg campaign and the battle that changed the course of America's Civil War. I have visited the battlefield many times and am always moved by the Cyclorama. Although Mr. Hall and Jason Andrews do not exist, the staff of the Gettysburg

National Military Park pointed me to digitized records containing information on the soldiers that fought the monumental battle. The names of the potential 'Toms' are fictional but other details regarding Ramseur's Brigade are accurate.

Confederates troops marched from Carlisle to Gettysburg through the community of Mt. Holly Springs. Robert Givin's papermill was already in operation in the summer of 1863 and when he died in 1879, his unmarried daughter Amelia took over the mill's management. She gave her community the library that bears her name in 1890.

Liza Mundy's 2017 book, *Code Girls: The Untold Story of American Women Code Breakers of World War II* tells the story of the important and complex work of these women. Amelia Calafont is modeled on the true women whose stories Mundy tells. They would have listened to the popular World War II love song, "I'll be seeing you." The music was written by Sammy Fain with lyrics by Irving Kahal in 1938.

Three special friends encouraged and advised me while writing this book. Robin Fidler and Sandi Boone read pages as they emerged and Cathy Gorn listened to me read passages. Pam Greer provided editorial expertise. But it is my husband, Jim Baker, who lived through the experience of the book's creation. He reminded me more than once that Tom, Amelia, and Callie live only in my mind.

Deborah Sweaney

Carlisle, PA

About the Illustrators

The art work in The Spirit of the Limestone House was created by students from the award-winning Carlisle Pennsylvania High School Art & Design Department, under the direction of Art & Design Department Chair Ashley Gogoj, and former chair, Melissa Gallagher.

Students submitted sample drawings, competing for the chance to illustrate this book. Passages were given to the students to trigger their creative juices, and Mrs. Gogoj and Mrs. Gallagher selected the winning entries. Three students were offered commissions and received a stipend for their work.

Madison Gould's drawing of a limestone house was chosen as the cover illustration. Madison calls herself "a military brat," who has grown up living in several different places, including Washington, D. C., Missouri, and Germany. She came to Carlisle when her father was stationed at the U.S. Army War College. Shortly after her high school graduation in 2019, her family moved to Utah. Madison will be attending Savannah College of Art and Design starting in the fall of 2019 and plans to major in animation and storyboarding.

Hailey Myers and Mabel Sheesley were selected to create the illustrations throughout the book. Each was commissioned to draw ten images.

Hailey is also a member of the Carlisle graduating class of 2019. She has always loved art, but realized her junior year of high school that she wanted to make a career of it. Throughout high school she was involved in the National Art Honor Society and was part of a team of students who painted and installed a mural in downtown Carlisle. She will be attending Tyler School of Art at Temple University in the fall of 2019 to study graphic design.

Mabel Sheesley will graduate from Carlisle High School in 2021. She is a proud member of the Student Council, the National Honor Society, and the Shakespeare Troupe. At a young age she began developing her creativity, starting with still life sketches and eventually focusing on painting varicolored figures. She loves the feeling of gratification when she can say "I finished my painting!" Mabel previously received an award from Artistic Expressions which resulted in her work being on display at the Susquehanna Art Museum.

Mrs. Gogoj mentored the students during the process, helping them to create just the right illustration to accompany a particular passage. Melissa Gallagher then merged the student's artwork with the text and laid out the book for publication.

About the Author

Like Callie Monroe in *The Spirit of the Limestone House*, Deborah Sweaney's life started in the Midwest. She grew up in Missouri across the river from Callie's Kansas, but like her heroine, life events took her to Washington, D.C. and the Cumberland Valley of Pennsylvania. Deborah captured her own story in her first three books: *Unpacking Memories, Up in the Air, and Blest Be the Tie.*

Her love of history shows throughout her writings, and her stories are always told against the backdrop of historic events. She has a special connection to the American Civil War for she met her husband of thirty-three years on a tour of Civil War forts. She now lives in Carlisle, Pennsylvania with her husband Jim, her dog Muffin, and a house full of books. *The Spirit of the Limestone House* is her first work of fiction.